Wimp no more

I felt a weird sensation, little prickles over my body. Dots of ice. I imagined chemo bubbles in my bloodstream and shivered. My senses seemed super-sharp. The hum of the electronic machines behind me was a tidal roar. I noticed tiny scratches on the glass of the mirror, smelled the chemicals in the indoor-outdoor carpet. Should I talk to Dr. Wallabini about this?

Dozens, scores, hundreds of icy specks blinked, a thousand icy prickles. Power surged through my body. I grabbed the barbell, the one with three hundred pounds of weight. The kid in the mirror said, Hit me with your best shot, wimp.

I threw the barbell into his stupid face. Smoothly, in one continuous fluid motion, I picked up the three hundred pounds and hurled it at the mirror.

The kid disappeared in an explosion of shattering glass.

Suddenly, all the strength drained out of my body. I was weak and dizzy. I sat down in a pool of chunky glass. I was never so scared in my life.

It was great.

ROBERT LIPSYTE
The Chemo Kid

HarperKeypoint
An Imprint of HarperCollins*Publishers*

Library of Congress Cataloging-in-Publication Data
Lipsyte, Robert.
    The Chemo Kid: a novel / by Robert Lipsyte.
        p.   cm.
    Summary: When the drugs that he takes as part of his chemotherapy
suddenly transform him from wimp into superhero, sixteen-year-old Fred
and his friends plot to rid the town of its most lethal environmental hazard,
toxic waste in the water supply.
    ISBN 0-06-020284-X. — ISBN 0-06-020285-8 (lib. bdg.)
    ISBN 0-06-447101-2 (pbk.)
    [1. Cancer—Fiction.   2. Environmental protection—Fiction.
3. Pollution—Fiction.   4. Self-confidence—Fiction.]   I. Title.
PZ7.L67Ch   1992   91-55500
[Fic]—dc20   CIP
                                                                                      AC

Harper Keypoint is an imprint of Harper Trophy, a division of HarperCollins
Publishers. First Harper Keypoint edition, 1993.

For all the chemo kids

1

WE WERE SLOW DANCING in a dim corner at the Junior Prom when Mara discovered the lump. I'd never been so close to a girl before. I could tell she liked me. I felt dreamy. My feet were moving to the music on their own, no connection to my head, which felt like a balloon bumping gently against the top of the world.

"Fred? What's this?" That tugged the string of my balloon.

"What's what?"

"This." Mara touched the left side of my neck. "Does it hurt you?"

Mara lifted my hand off her waist and guided it

up to a spot below my earlobe.

The lump was just under the skin, firm to the touch, as big as an egg.

That popped my balloon. I felt stupid before I felt scared. Of all nights to grow a lump. She'd think I was a jerk.

"It's nothing," I said. "Doesn't even hurt."

My feet lost the beat, but I waited until the song ended and the DJ started to rap before I excused myself. There was a crowd of guys in the back of the restaurant outside the bathroom, puffing cigarettes and plotting the rest of the evening. Reservoir runs. Caravans down to the Shore. I should have wondered why they weren't inside the bathroom, but I was concentrating on wiggling through the crowd, my left hand over the lump, hoping no one would notice me. As usual. Of course, the one time you don't want to be noticed, you get spotted right away.

"Don't go in there," someone shouted.

My right hand was on the bathroom door when Jeff Wise grabbed it. "It's hell in there. Tank and Roger are facing off." Jeff was sucking in his chubby cheeks for that anchorman look, so I knew I couldn't believe him.

I kept going.

"Don't do it." Jon Park hadn't been the same since a cheerleader told him he looked like a Korean Elvis Presley. But Jon always told the truth, even if it hurt. Someone else. "Tank and Roger said anyone who goes in would come out with a different face. Probably even someone as harmless as you."

"Got to go," I said.

"Try to hold it," said Jeff. "You could get crushed in The Final Confrontation."

"Makes no sense," I said. "They always fight in public—they love audiences."

Tank Ganz was captain of the football team, an all-state linebacker, and Roger Sharkey was the school dope dealer and the Mayor's nephew. They owned Nearmont High. They hated each other, but except for some noise at major events like the Prom, they pretty much left each other alone. No one could understand why. They should have had their big showdown years ago.

I imagined the lump growing under my hand, turning colors. I took my hand off it to push the bathroom door. I had to see it.

One of the guys saw it first. "A hickey already? What'd she use, a vacuum cleaner?" Guys laughed and repeated the line.

Someone else shouted, "It's the king zit from hell."

Suddenly I was in the middle of a swarm. Everybody had a comment. Even Jeff. "Alien parasite at the Prom. Tape at eleven." Some friend.

"A swollen gland," announced Jon Park. He knew everything. "Could be nothing, could be fatal."

Now I had to see it immediately. I pushed into

the bathroom. It was hot and damp and smoky. It took a moment for my eyes to adjust, and then I couldn't believe what I saw.

Tank Ganz and a line of football players were leaning against one white tile wall, their tuxedo pants down around their ankles, their butts exposed in the bright fluorescent lights.

They were passing around a bottle and howling while Roger Sharkey and his twin goons were jabbing hypodermic needles into their white and pink and brown backsides.

There was a little medical station on top of a trash can, syringes, tiny bottles, alcohol swabs. I saw a pile of cash.

Whatever was going on, I had the feeling I shouldn't be seeing it.

Too late now. I headed straight for the mirrors. The skin over the lump was paler than the rest of my neck, as if it was being stretched thin by the egg trying to break through. I tapped it. No pain.

"What are you doing in here?" Tank's voice bounced off the tile walls and slapped against my face. "Get 'im."

In the mirror, I saw the football team pull up their pants and start toward me.

"Whoaaa," said Roger Sharkey. "Just the wrong boy. In the wrong place. At the wrong time." He always talked in half sentences.

Roger glided through the team along a path his twin goons cleared for him. He moved so smoothly he could have been on roller blades. He was tall and thin, the only white kid in school with a mustache. It divided his pale face like a hyphen drawn by a Magic Marker. He gave me the creeps.

"Leave him to me," ordered Tank Ganz.

"This is business," said Roger.

"My turf," said Tank.

"This restaurant. Is not school property," said Roger. A goon appeared on either side of him and nodded.

"It is tonight," said Tank. The football players formed a huddle behind him.

I held my breath. I was right in the middle of the action. If this was a football game, I'd be the center. Great position.

"This is not. A game," said Roger. "We can win. Without violence." He plucked two plastic Baggies out of his double-breasted white jacket. There were crooked little cigarettes in one Baggie, colored pills in the other. "Your choice. To ice you down."

"Uh, thanks. I'm cool." I knew I didn't sound cool. My mouth was dry. I touched the lump without thinking about it. Still there. Could be nothing.

"Roger's treat," said Roger. "The Prom. A time. For you to get happy at last."

"You don't have to bribe the little nerd," said Tank.

"A gift," said Roger. "To make him one of us. Do you want him. Telling everybody what he saw?"

"We'll do this my way," growled Tank. "When we're through, he won't even remember his name."

5

"What is your name?" asked Roger.

"Fred Bauer."

"Fred," said Roger, "you can't go through life. Scared of chemicals." He held up the Baggies.

"Fred," snarled Tank. "Just say no."

I couldn't believe what was happening. Not real life. A dream, a TV movie, the start of a new Cyber-Punk Rovers adventure? Did I slip through a wormhole into a secondary universe, did I flashmail myself into an outlaw program?

Get real, Fred, for the first time in your life you're front row center at LIFE. And this is the moment everybody's been waiting for since Tank and Roger divided up Nearmont High. It's the final confrontation.

"Fred?" asked Roger, shaking the Baggies.

"Fred," said Tank, shaking his head.

I'd never been the center of attention before. I wasn't sure if I liked it or not. My palms were wet, but that was nothing new. My knees quivered.

What was I supposed to do? I couldn't take one of the Baggies. Tank and the team would be on my case until graduation. Another year.

I couldn't just say no. Sharkey and his goons would make my life miserable. For starters.

I could just do nothing at all and wait to see who would get me first. Typical Fred Bauer. If this was a football game, I'd be the football.

"Fred?"

"Fred?"

They weren't even looking at me anymore. They were eyeball to eyeball. The showdown.

Roger blinked first.

"I cannot believe this," he said. "World War Three. About to start. Over the invisible boy. Mr. Nobody."

"Don't try to weasel your way out," growled Tank.

"You know what they'll write about Fred? In the yearbook?" Roger waited a beat. "'He was here. We think.'"

Everybody laughed except Tank and me.

Tank said to Roger, "Hit the road, toad."

Roger said to Tank, "If you were really so tough you wouldn't need the steroid shots."

The laughter gurgled away. It was suddenly very quiet in the bathroom. The dripping faucets sounded like the ticking of time bombs.

Tank grabbed my right arm. Roger grabbed my left.

"Get your hands. Off him," said Roger.

"You let go," said Tank.

They began to pull. A hot wire of pain started in my wrists and ran into my chest. They were going to pull me apart.

"Break it up." A voice as snarly as a classroom buzzer echoed off the bathroom tiles. Everyone scurried out of the way as Coach Burg, his varsity "N" cap perched on his big head, swaggered in. "What's going on here?" He was glaring at me.

The crowd of guys had burst in behind him. I saw Jeff and Jon, their eyes wide, their mouths open, like everybody else's.

The football players were hiding bottles in the trash cans, and the goons were stuffing money and needles into their pockets. Roger and Tank dropped my arms and pushed me at Coach Burg. I had the feeling Coach Burg was focusing so hard on me so he wouldn't have to deal with the football star and the Mayor's nephew, who were already easing out the door.

"What's your name?"

"Fred Bauer?" Did I sound like I wasn't sure?

"Where do you go to school?"

"I'm a junior here?"

"How come I haven't seen you before?"

"The lump," said Jeff, "has changed his appearance."

"Jefferson Wise," said Coach Burg, "how long do you think you'll be editor of the paper if I keep finding you in questionable situations?"

"He's got to cover the news," said Jon.

"Jonathan Park," said Coach Burg. "Captain of the Computer Team won't mean zip to a college that gets a bad character reference from me."

"Fred's our friend," said Jeff. "Look at his neck."

Coach Burg slipped on half glasses to study the lump. "Leave it alone. Maybe it'll go away."

"Maybe it'll go away," said Jon. "Those are the four most dangerous words in the English language."

"That's actually five words," said Jeff. "Unless you count a contraction as one word."

"You're talking syntax, I'm talking survival," said Jon.

"Words are the greatest weapons in the world," said Jeff.

"You boys come to the Prom to dance or do philosophy?" snarled Coach Burg. "Get out there quick or everyone goes home early. And take Ed with you."

They grabbed my sore arms and hustled me out of the bathroom. I realized it was the first time the three of us had done something together since the good old CyberPunk Rovers days in my basement.

I had to tell them. "Roger and the twins were giving Tank and the players steroid injections."

"The game is over," snapped Jeff. "Grow up."

"There is a very thin line," said Jon coldly, "between fantasy and insanity." They let me go.

Mara was waiting outside the bathroom. She looked worried. "You okay?"

"It was close," said Jon. "They might have torn Fred apart."

"Why?"

"He was just a symbol," said Jeff. "At that moment, whoever controlled Fred Bauer controlled the soul of Nearmont High. Hey, that's good." He fumbled inside his tuxedo jacket for his pen and notebook.

"I'm confused," said Mara.

"I'll tell you later," I said. "Let's dance."

I led her back to our dim corner in time for an-

9

other slow number, but my feet never found the beat again. Even when I forgot about the lump for a few minutes, a couple would cruise by to catch a glimpse of the invisible boy who almost started World War Three.

I had to get out of there. I wracked my brain for some smooth way to suggest to Mara that we make a reservoir run. I'd never been there with a girl. I tried to remember some of the cool lines I'd heard guys use.

Like, How about we check out the whales?

I knew that wouldn't sound right coming from me.

I was still working on my line when the slow dance ended and Mara said, "It's such a nice night. Why don't we drive down to the reservoir?"

2

I COULDN'T TELL IF the moon's face was smiling encouragement or mocking me. Or just saying, Move closer, dork. Put your arm around her.

The moon hung pale and fat over the reservoir, casting an eerie light that skimmed the silver water and splashed into the cars parked along the fence. The light made Mara's face older, more mysterious. I felt hot and cold.

I tried to think of something clever to say. Finally, I said, "Better call Stephen King."

"Who?"

"You know. The writer. All those scary stories."

"Why?"

"Well, uh, the light?" I felt dumb. "Isn't it sort of, uh, spooky? The way it rises off the water?"

"That's the baronium," said Mara. "And it is scary. Especially if you drink it."

"We all drink that water."

"That's why it's scary. Can you see the building on the other side of the reservoir?"

Through the high chain-link fence, across the silvery water and through an even higher and thicker metal fence, I could just barely make out the shape of a squat, brown, concrete building. Actually, I wasn't sure I was seeing it so much as remembering it. I'd driven past it hundreds of times, never thinking about it much. "What about it?"

"The baronium might be coming from that building. We've been talking about it at the Ecology Club. I'm trying to get those wimps to stage an action."

"An action?"

"We've got to find out what's going on in that building. The Mayor won't tell us. The police say it's none of our business."

"What kind of an action?"

"We need to sneak in there and get samples and photographs." She sounded very determined and stern. "And maybe plug the pipes if we have to."

"Isn't that illegal?" I sounded wimpy.

"Leaking baronium into our water supply is illegal. You should come to meetings."

12

"Yeah, well, uh . . ." I had no excuses. I knew I should be interested in that stuff, but it had never seemed like you could do anything about it. And nobody had ever invited me before.

"Every Wednesday. We could use some of your cold fire."

"My what?"

"You remember." Her voice sounded warmer now, softer. "What you said in Myth in Literature."

"Oh, that." I squirmed around in the driver's seat. The one time I had shot my mouth off in English class.

"I really liked what you said." She cocked her head and closed her eyes. She was beautiful in the light, even if it was baronium. "You said, 'Most people are just empty Styrofoam burger boxes floating along the storm drains of life, but the hero is a person with a cold fire—a seeker with the fiery, passionate righteousness to complete the journey and the cool, confident skills to triumph.' That was so excellent."

"Yeah, well . . ." How could I ever tell her I had remembered that from the Heroes chapter of the CyberPunk Rovers Playbook?

"I knew you must be smart, that you read a lot about myths, but you know the real reason I liked you, the reason I asked you to the Prom?"

All I really knew right then was that I really didn't want to know the real reason.

13

"Because you said that the hero was a 'person.' That means male or female. Most boys just don't get that."

The Playbook had read, "The hero is a creature . . ." I had changed one word. I knew I'd better change the subject.

"So, what are you going to do this summer?"

"GreenAction Leadership camp." She moved closer to me. For the first time I was glad I didn't have bucket seats. "Somebody in this town has to learn how to break something."

"Break something?"

"That's Greenie talk for fighting back against polluters and dumpers and greedheads. It's symbolic, but sometimes you really do have to go out and break something so they know you won't stand for your planet being poisoned."

"Break something." I felt bold enough to slip my arm behind her head and across her shoulders. She snuggled in to me.

"What are you doing this summer?"

"My dad wants me to work for him, learn the stock, make some deliveries."

"Are you interested in computer software?"

"Not particularly, but I don't have any other ideas yet." I shrugged, a carefully planned gesture that got me even closer. I could feel the heat from her cheek.

"You should come to camp with me."

"Be great," I said. Our lips were very close.

Mara raised her hand to my face. I couldn't tell if she was about to draw me closer or push me away.

I never found out.

"Oh." She touched the lump. "I'm sorry."

"No. It's nothing." But all the good hot and cold feelings drained away and I felt a toothache in my stomach and something scarier than the mist off the reservoir began to cloud my brain.

After a little while, I said I wasn't feeling well and I drove Mara home.

3

OUR FAMILY DOCTOR SAID, "Swollen gland, could be nothing. But I'd like to run some tests. Strictly routine."

"What could it be if it's something?" Mom was on the other side of the examining room curtain. Her voice was high, almost squeaky, the way it gets when she's nervous.

The doctor said, "Let's talk while Frank gets dressed."

"Fred," squeaked Mom.

"Of course." The doctor winked at me and walked through the curtain. "It doesn't seem so long ago you had to carry him in here."

Might have to carry me out. I felt glued to the examining table. Sore all over from the doctor's pinching and poking. Even the lump hurt now. My throat was closing up. My fingers crumpled the paper sheet.

I caught my reflection in the glass doors of a medicine cabinet, a naked kid who wasn't fat, wasn't thin, was just here, we think.

Mom was at the reception desk, paying the bill and making another appointment. She flashed her fake smile. "Let's do some ice cream."

"At ten o'clock in the morning?"

"Chill out, dude."

"No one says that anymore."

"But they still scarf up Mojave Desert pecan crunch."

The ice cream had no taste, but we sat in the car pretending to enjoy it.

"Why can't they do the tests right away?" I sounded whiney.

"There's a waiting list."

"That big of a deal?" I sounded scared.

"That routine. Everybody has them done. Look, Freddy, if he thought it was serious, he'd slap you right into the hospital."

"If it's not serious, why bother?" I stopped listening to myself.

"We'd better get home," she said, starting the car. "You'll miss afternoon classes."

"I've got a medical excuse. I can take the day off."

"Spring term, junior year, is key. You can't let down now."

"I won't go to college anyway if I'm dying or something."

"Don't you talk like that," she squeaked. She nearly ran a red light. "Look what you made me do."

"Chill out, dude." We both laughed. Somehow, saying the word dying made me feel better, like spitting out a sour pit.

"Uh-oh, the cops," said Mom, still laughing. A Nearmont patrol car pulled up alongside us, its cherry-top light flashing. I could see Sergeant Durie, the grouchy traffic cop, glaring at us. He was just about to say something when his radio crackled and he took off.

"That was a boo," said Mom. She gave me her fake grin. "Like your lump. Just a scare."

The phone was ringing when we got home. Dad wanted to know about the doctor's visit. Mom waited until I started upstairs before she began mumbling into the phone. I overheard words. Specialist. City. Bloodwork. Scans.

I searched through my drawers for a turtleneck shirt to cover the lump. I didn't want to be talking about it at school this afternoon. I remembered I had once left one down in the basement for chilly winter afternoons playing The Game.

It was in the bottom of the cedar closet with the stack of demonstration computer games Dad had brought home one day for me and my friends to try out. That's what had gotten us started. Most of the games were boring, but CyberPunk Rovers grabbed us right away. The adventures took place in a high-tech future run by multinational corporations that killed for information. If you weren't working for one of them or hooked up with the Stilyagi, the largest international crime organization, you were probably living in a Squat, one of the shantytowns of New Osaka or New Budapest or New Nairobi.

Unless, of course, you were a CyberPunk Rover, a hustler operating on the Edge, slipping in and out of dangerous deals with the corporations and the Stilyagi, sometimes working for both at the same time.

Those were good times. Got us through middle school. Other kids played, but Jeff and Jon and I were the regulars. We went on adventures that lasted for weeks. We'd play on Saturdays and Sundays and after school. Mom and Dad didn't like it after a while, but they were glad I had friends. One summer weekend we played nonstop except to sleep sitting up on the old cracked brown leather couch. That might have been the time I finally came up with Ranger.

Jon had already invented his character, Ace, the computer cowboy who could crack into any network in the world, a mercenary with a bionic arm that plugged right into his deck.

Jeff was Scribe, master of the media, a TV newshound who bought and sold hot information, most of which he made up in a show called the Scribe Report.

I tried a few different roles, industrial spy and astronaut and even a politician, but nothing really fit until I came up with Ranger. Jeff and Jon thought he was square, a white-hat hero in a world of grays, but I felt good being on the right side. And I never felt like a nobody when I played The Game.

I was the GameMaster. I planned the adventures and invented the minor characters, like Splicer, the dwarf medic who would install stolen organs and synthetic eyes for a fee; the Mutant Pack, a gang of cyborgs and genetic freaks who could be your best friends or your worst enemies, depending on how they felt that day, and Bang, the cop who had a grudge against Rovers.

My favorite minor character was Scattergood, a mysterious girl who roamed the planet helping kids in trouble. Ranger was in love with her. Sometimes I thought I was too.

During freshman year, when Jeff got on the school paper and Jon discovered girls, we started playing only on weekends, and after a while The Game just sort of drifted away. I never found anything to replace it that made me as happy. I loved being the GameMaster.

I was feeling so sorry for myself, I didn't hear Mom come down the stairs.

"Hey, " she said softly, "let's take the day off. We'll catch a flick, talk. I know you've got lots on your mind."

I didn't want to deal with that. "Got to get to school." I shoved the CyberPunk stuff back into the closet. "Spring term, junior year, is key."

4

THE TURTLENECK WAS TOO warm for June, but no one paid me any attention in history or French. As usual. My plan was to sit alone and eat fast in a corner of the cafeteria, but Mara spotted me and waved me over to a seat she had saved at a table with Jon and Joanie Kim. I was surprised Mara was still talking to me after the Prom.

"What did the doctor say?"

"Strictly routine. Tests."

"Don't start to panic," said Jon, "until you wake up shivering in the middle of the night, feverish, chilled, soaked in a pool of your own sweat."

"What'll that mean?" I started to panic.

"It could mean a chronic systemic disease. Like—"

"Newsbreaker!" Jeff stormed up to the table, his usual dramatics. It was the way he had played The Game. "Roger and Tank. Interested?"

"No," said Jon, paging through a textbook. It was the way he had played The Game. Never let them think you care.

"Go on," I said. My role was to keep things rolling.

"Scene." Jeff took a noisy swig of Joanie's diet soda. She giggled. "After the Prom. A dark, moonless night . . ."

"There's always a moon," said Jon, "even if you can't see it."

". . . and Tank is trailing Roger all the way down to Shorehaven. Tank's in the Bronco trying to run Roger's Beamer off the highway." Jeff took a long, noisy swig of Mara's bottled water. I was glad to see she frowned at that. "They drive out on the beach. Scene. It's dawn, the sun rising out of the Atlantic Ocean . . ."

"No moon and a wet sun," said Jon. "There's a story."

". . . as Tank and Roger face off. They're silhouetted in the early light, Tank swinging a baseball bat, Roger his knife and ninja stars."

"You were that close?" asked Joanie breathlessly.

"This is from sources," said Jeff. "You want more?"

"No," said Jon.

"Go on," I said.

"They come closer and closer, trying to maneuver each other into the blinding light of the rising sun. Tank chokes up on his bat, Roger cocks a ninja star.

"Suddenly Roger says, 'This is crazy, Tank. We shouldn't be. Fighting over a nobody.' And Tank says, 'For once you're right, Roger. Fred Bauer's the problem.'" Jeff collapsed into a plastic cafeteria chair, gasping for breath. "They left that Shorehaven summit promising to work out their Bauer problem together. By any means necessary."

There were other kids around by this time. One of them said, "This was on TV last night?"

"The Scribe Report," I said. "Everything but the truth."

"Maybe you have better information," said Jeff. He winked at Jon. "Injections."

"Did you ask them to come to your basement and play The Game?" sneered Jon.

Mara was looking at me quizzically, and I was trying to think of what to say, when Joanie asked, "So what happened?"

"Nothing," said Jeff.

"I hope they never come back to school," said Mara. "Creeps."

The kids around the table got quiet, and some of them edged away. That's how scared people were of Tank and Roger.

"Look how they've intimidated everybody," said

Mara. I felt proud of the way she plunged on, but a little nervous, too. "They run the school like two warlords."

"Not bad," said Jeff, fishing for his pen. "Tank and Roger, astride Nearmont High like medieval warlords."

"Get real." She sounded angry now. "They're no heroes, a sleazy dope pusher and a jock animal who likes to hurt people."

"If they're so bad," said Joanie, "why don't they get kicked out?"

"Because they keep the rest of us in line," said Mara. "They're gangsters, and Coach Burg is part of that gang, and the Mayor, and all of us if we let them get away with it."

"That is total paranoia," said Jon.

My mind must have been still in the CyberPunk basement, because I said, "It's the Nearmont Stilyagi."

"Stilyagi?" asked Mara.

"From a stupid game we used to play," said Jon.

"Only Freddy took it seriously," said Jeff. He was still annoyed by my Scribe Report crack. "Ranger never quit, but Ranger always died."

"Ranger?" asked Mara.

"He lived by the Heroes' Creed," sneered Jeff.

Mara looked interested. "What's that?"

It just rolled out of me. "Do No Harm for Profit." I could see it in boldface on the first page of the Heroes chapter of the Playbook, the shortest chapter. "Protect the Needy. Always Choose Right over Wrong."

"That's beautiful," said Mara.

"That's babytalk," said Jon. "There's no right or wrong, there's only what works and what doesn't."

Mara smiled at me. "Fred doesn't buy that, do you?"

I was trying to frame an answer when a voice snarled, "Turtleneck in June? You hiding a hickey?" Coach Burg chuckled to himself and swaggered away.

"He didn't remember you," said Jon.

"Without your lump," said Jeff, "you're just another face in the crowd.

"Freddy, you're shivering."

They finally trapped Ranger in the Chasm, whacked him with enough juice to fry the Mutant Pack and stapled him to a radioactive dump. Ace and Scribe laughed as his sweat bubbled in the murderous air.

"Don!" squeaked Mom. "Hurry up!"

I woke up burning with fever, chilled from soaking in a pool of sweat.

5

DON'T REMEMBER one clear thought in the next couple of weeks, just quick images on a video screen of car rides, whispered conversations, white coats, Mom squeaking, cold X-ray plates pressed against my chest, nurses chirping "Sharp stick!" just before they stuck another needle into my finger, which surprisingly hurt more than the needles they stuck into my arm or the hole they cut in my instep so blue dye could be squirted through my system and tracked while I lay in a dark, humming tunnel of steel. I remember the expression on my parents' faces when I woke up after the operation to cut the lump out of my neck. They were trying

27

too hard to smile. I knew the diagnosis was bad. But I wasn't afraid. It all seemed unreal, a Cyber-Punk Rovers adventure. No matter what happened on the journey, you could always walk upstairs from the basement into the warmth of the kitchen.

The only doctor I remember from those days and nights was very short, and he had an enormous head topped with a bush of curly gray hair. His skin was dark and his eyes were soft and brown. He had an accent.

"Hello, Frad. I am Dr. Wallabini."

"Am I going to die?"

"Of course. We will all die. But you, not so soon, I think." Something steady about him gave me confidence.

"Do I have . . . cancer?"

"Absolutely. A very rare form that moves rapidly. We removed the original malignancy"—he touched the bandage on the left side of my neck—"leaving a scar that will someday look like a wrinkle. We can't be sure that some cancer didn't already break away. We have chemotherapy drugs to go after those cells, seek them out and destroy them."

"Will it hurt?"

"There may be side effects—nausea and vomiting, fatigue, swelling. Hair loss."

"Can you cure me?"

"Not without your help."

"My help?"

"You are not a mere spectator at a contest be-tween cancer cells and killer drugs. Your attitude is important. Your will to get healthy. People give up; sometimes it seems easier to die than hang in there, go the distance." He squeezed my big toe through the bedsheet. "You've got to be your own hero. People need to find things inside themselves they never knew were there."

When my head finally cleared, I saw plastic bags swaying and swishing. They hung upside down from a metal rack over my bed. For hours, I watched the fluids in the bags drip down through clear tubes and into the silver needles embedded in the veins of my forearms.

There was no pain. But as each droplet rolled through a needle and entered a vein, I felt a cold prickle. I shivered as specks of ice sailed along my bloodstream, then disappeared somewhere in my body, killer drugs on the trail of cancer cells.

Mom was wrestling a piece of cardboard taller than she was into my room. "It's a get-well card. From the Junior Class."

"Mara brought it over," said Dad. There were deep lines in his forehead and around his mouth I had never seen before.

"Mara's so nice," said Mom. "She wants to visit."

"No!" It came out before I thought about it.

"She really likes you," said Mom.

"Don't nag him," said Dad.

"It's not nagging," said Mom. "It's for him."

"Then let him decide."

I'd never heard them snap at each other before. I felt sorry for them. They had a sick kid in the hospital.

"I'm sorry, Don." Mom reached over and touched Dad's arm. "Nerves."

Dad looked sheepish. "I'm sorry, Sue. Sorry, Fred."

My lips were actually forming the words "No Problem" when the first wave of nausea bubbled up from my stomach in a hot stream of lava. I closed my mouth just in time.

"Nurse!" yelled Mom.

My body began to vibrate. Nurses ran in. They rolled me over on my side and held a plastic bucket under my face.

Long after there was no more food or water inside me to throw up, I shuddered with dry heaves that turned my throat into a fiery desert and filled my mouth with sand. My chest was burning, my belly was a twisted towel, my eyes were stinging balls pushing out of their sockets. My bones ached. Even my hair hurt.

I felt like I was trying to vomit out my lungs.

The nurses stroked my forehead. After a while, exhausted, I stopped heaving long enough to collapse and sleep. I dreamed of The Game.

Splicer was out there somewhere, and the Mutant Pack, tuned to the errant blips in the grid that signaled Ranger in danger. Have to focus, have to concentrate, have to send the message for help.

6

"**I** WANT TO SEE YOU before I go." Mara's voice on the telephone sounded far away. Nearmont was another planet.

"I don't think so."

"Why not?"

"It's a weird place—you wouldn't like it."

"I'm coming to see you, not the hospital."

"I'll think about it."

"There isn't much time left."

"Anything new in school?"

"Not to change the subject." Mara sighed. "One more final. And the Myth paper's due Thursday. Jeff gave me a good idea for it." I felt a stab of jealousy until she added, "He said to ask you about Ranger."

"You're not doing a paper on The Game?"

"No, on the similarities among heroes in different cultures. Like Prometheus, Buddha, King Arthur. Jeff said Ranger was more like a traditional hero than a CyberPunk character."

"That's why I always lost."

"Jeff said you wouldn't let Ranger cut shady deals."

"He was kind of square, Ranger." I liked talking to her about The Game. "Sometimes I . . ."

That was as far as I got before my body started vibrating again and a fuzzy fist reached up from my stomach into my throat. "Gotta go."

I slammed down the receiver just before the hot lava came up, and the heaves began. No one had told me it would be back so soon.

A creature swung into my room on crutches. Bald as an egg, big blue eyes, one leg. Could have been a member of the Mutant Pack. It said, "Hey, fresh meat. Whatcha in for?"

"Cancer."

"Duh." The creature screwed a bony finger into a pale cheek. "We all got cancer here, dip. The whole floor. The entire building. Okay, let's go, time for shrink-rap."

"Shrink-rap?"

"Group therapy. Wallabini's Weenies. Can you walk?"

"Sure." I tried to slide my legs out of bed but they were concrete slabs. I felt a stab of terror. Paralyzed.

"Relax. Just temporary. I'll get a nurse." The creature swung out, shaking its head.

Two nurses hoisted me into a wheelchair and pushed me and the chemo rack through a corridor of kids, some of them teenagers, some toddlers, with tubes coming out of their arms, their noses, their necks. Most of them were wearing T-shirts and jeans. A lot of baseball caps. I had to get out of this hospital gown. Sunlight flooded through the windows of rooms we passed.

Every few feet we rolled through another sound zone: rap, hard core, heavy metal, even country. A bunch of kids were watching a soap in a recreation room that opened onto a small terrace that over-looked New York harbor.

They wheeled me into Dr. Wallabini's office. He was sitting behind an enormous desk piled with pa-pers and computer equipment. Only his big, curly gray-haired head showed above the desk. Facing him were four kids around my age in straight-backed wooden chairs. The bald, one-legged crea-ture was wearing a bra under her volleyball-team T-shirt. It was a girl.

"Here comes Mr. Excitement," she said.

"Let's welcome Frad," said Dr. Wallabini. He pointed a stubby little finger at the creature. "This is Spike. And that's Vandal." An unshaven guy with rings in his ears and a blue bandanna wrapped around his head curled his lip at me. "Brian." A black kid in a jogging suit and an LA Raiders cap flashed a peace sign. "Alison." A pretty girl in a white turban smiled.

They all looked me over for a moment and lost interest. I felt myself disappearing.

"I should tell you, Frad," said Dr. Wallabini, "we are working on our individual mental images of the drugs as they seek and destroy cancer cells. It's part of maintaining a positive attitude. Shall we give Frad a sample? Anyone?"

Alison tipped her head back. "I see a white light." She had a sweet, breathless voice. "A beam of white light, powerful in its purity because it comes from the thoughts of all those who love me. It moves through every nook and cranny of my body. Anything it touches becomes clean."

"It could do my laundry," said Spike.

"This is a *support* group," said Dr. Wallabini.

"Yo," said Vandal. "My chemo's a greaseball biker posse, fifty hardballs on king hell hogs running down the cancer cells, which are all soft little debs who need to get hurt." He snickered through his nose at Alison. "Can you get your arms around that?"

"Of course," said Alison sweetly. "Whatever you need to get yourself well is beautiful."

"You think so too?" Vandal glared at me.

I tried to think of something to say, "Well, uh . . ."

I was back in the bathroom with Tank and Roger.

"Boy just landed," said Brian. "Give him space."

"You his mother?" Vandal sneered at Brian. "Mother."

"I didn't realize you had brain cancer too," said Brian, smoothly. He winked at me. "Visualize my band, Oil Slick, pouring sound through my veins, gospel honey smothering those ugly little cancer cells, jazz riffs splitting them apart, hard shafts of nasty rap knocking them dead."

"Good, good," said Dr. Wallabini. "Spike?"

"It's the finals, me on one side of the net, thousands of them on the other." She stood up on her one leg and brought her fist down. "Smash—every time I drill the ball into one of them, smash, it's one less cancer cell."

"Let's hear from Fred," said Alison. She smiled at me. She was very pretty.

"Well, uh . . ." The only image that popped into my head was Ranger, struggling against the staples that held him to the dump.

"Frad is in the middle of his first infusion," said Dr. Wallabini.

"I think he's in the middle of nowhere," said Vandal. "In the back of the pack with his thumb up his nose. A zero."

"He'll get smarter when his hair falls out," said Spike.

"I am glad we are so creative today," said Dr. Wallabini. He seemed to be slipping under his desk.

I could see only his head now, down to his nose. "But I wonder if it would not be more productive to focus on cancer cells as the enemy rather than each other."

Jeff and Jon called in the late afternoon from the speakerphone in the Parks' computer room. "So what's it like there?"

"It's like high school only you vomit more."

It took them a few seconds to figure out they were supposed to laugh. They did it nervously. Then Jeff said, "Mara's been bugging us to talk you into letting her visit before she leaves."

"I'll think about it."

"She likes you," said Jon.

I changed the subject. "What's up with Tank and Roger?"

"They're around," said Jeff.

"They say anything about me?"

Jeff's voice shifted gears. "That report was only a first draft."

"He made it up," said Jon. "No chase, no fight on the beach, no summit meeting to decide to get you."

"It's something brand-new," said Jeff. "Be very big someday. I call it a pre-creation. It could have happened."

"Sounds like the Scribe Report all right," I said coolly. But I wondered if maybe they changed the story so I wouldn't worry. "What did happen?"

"A little yelling in the parking lot," said Jeff. "Roger's going around saying that Tank gets his muscles out of a bottle. I guess he means the booze."

I thought of the tiny bottles on the trash can. Steroids.

"Mara wants the school to crack down on those guys," said Jon.

"You been talking to her a lot?" I felt that jealous stab again.

"Mostly about you," said Jeff. "Call her. Let her visit."

"I said I'd think about it."

I was thinking about it later when Mara walked into my room.

7

"**Y**OU SEEM . . . DIFFERENT," said Mara. We were sitting together on the wooden bench on the little terrace off the rec room. I'd been able to get out of bed without help, but I couldn't walk without holding on to the rolling metal chemo rack. Mara was making a major effort not to stare at the rack or the swinging bags or the tubes dangling out of my arms.

She seemed shy. How was I different?

"Lost weight," I said. It was late afternoon. The sun was dropping behind the skyscrapers. Made them look like hypodermic needles bathed in blood. Must be different to think of that.

"Not just looks. You seem, I don't know, older, wiser?"

"Everybody wants to think you get something positive out of cancer." She winced at the word. "So, when are you leaving?"

"Trying to get rid of me already?" She forced a laugh. I wished I could think of a cool way to tell her it was all right to check out the chemo apparatus, that I'd be glad to explain it.

"I mean to Greenpeace."

"GreenAction. It's a different group. More confrontational."

"Break something."

"Right." She smiled and seemed to relax a little. "You remembered."

"You psyched to go?"

"Sort of." She made a comic face. "I know this sounds goofy, but I feel like I'm running out on you."

"Really?" I felt warm. "Well, you could always call, send me postcards."

"We'll be in the woods most of the time."

"Messages by pigeon."

She laughed more than the line was worth. "When do you go home?"

"Maybe next weekend. I have to come back every week for tests, and every six weeks for chemo." I lifted my arms and waved the tubes. "It's not as bad as it looks."

She blinked hard. "You'll miss a lot of school."

40

"Mom talked to them. They said they'd cut me some slack."

"I'll help you. We can do homework together."

"Be great."

We sat in silence for a while. Finally, she said, "So, I'll be back in a month."

"Be great." This was getting dumb.

"Hey," she said, "I hope you don't think I'm too pushy. The Halloween Dance? Will you go with me?"

I closed my mouth before I said "Be great" again. I had the feeling she'd done it to make me feel good. It made me feel bad. The Halloween Dance was four months away. I read once about someone giving a dying person a ten-year diary as a show of confidence. This seemed like the same sort of thing.

Suddenly, I did feel different. From her. In here, we all had cancer, but out in her world I'd be a marked man, a scarlet "C" on my forehead. Like a varsity cap for a team of losers.

"So is it a date?"

She looked so sincere. I just said, "Be great."

More silence. The sun was almost gone. The sky behind the buildings darkened. We heard music from the rec room.

"So, uh, what are the other kids like?"

"Kids."

"I mean, are they nice, or . . ."

"It's like high school. Some are, some aren't. Cancer doesn't make you different. Except maybe to other people."

"I didn't mean you were, like, different, but . . ."

"Might look different. Alison looks like a model. A bald model." I was babbling. "Chemo usually makes your hair fall out."

"Will your, uh . . ."

"The stuff I'm taking, I'll probably lose my hair. Might get sores in my mouth. Hard to talk or eat or anything. One of the drugs makes your face puff out. Who knows? My skin might turn yellow or green." I wondered if I was some kind of sadist. I was enjoying the widening of her eyes, the quivering of her lips.

"It's just temporary, though, isn't it?"

"Most of the time. Say, if you want to change your mind about Halloween, it's all right."

"No, I don't, I . . ."

"I mean I'd understand your not wanting to go out with somebody who doesn't need a mask."

She bit her lip. "Why are you doing this?"

Why am I giving her such a hard time? "Doing what?"

"Giving me such a hard time."

"Yo, Fred. Quit giving her such a hard time." Vandal stomped out onto the terrace. He was wearing heavy black boots, black jeans, and a black leather motorcycle jacket without sleeves. He had a plastic chemo bag draped on each shoulder as if they were some kind of gang insignia. Tubes

42

snaked out of the chemo bags into the needles in his forearms. "Weed?" He shook a cigarette out of a pack and held it out to Mara.

"No, thanks." She frowned. "Should you be smoking?"

"Should be smoking reefer."

I said, "There's no smoking on this floor."

"Whatsa matter, 'fraid you'll get cancer?" He laughed through his nose. "Frai-dee." Behind Vandal, through the glass doors of the rec room, I could see Brian and Spike and Alison watching us. "You gonna introduce me?"

"Mara." I never heard my voice so tiny before. "Vandal."

"Some place, huh?" He tapped his cigarette on the back of his hand. "I call it 'C' City. Folks are dyin' to get in, dyin' to get out." He pointed the cigarette at the ten-foot fence around the terrace. "Make sure we don't take the big dive."

"Fred?" Mara looked pale.

Vandal licked the cigarette tip before he put it in his mouth. He raised a Zippo lighter to the tip of his cigarette. "Frai-dee?"

I knew I was supposed to do something. I was being pulled again. "Can't you read the No Smoking sign?" My voice sounded squeaky.

Vandal flipped back the lid of the lighter with a crack that sounded like a pistol shot. "So what are you going to do?"

Do? I could leap up, stride across the terrace,

knock the lighter out of his hand and slam him to the ground. In one continuous motion. What any hero with cold fire would do.

"Nothing, that's what you'll do." He thumbed the lighter into flame. "Because you're a wimp."

The terrace door banged open. Spike growled, "You light that butt, we'll light yours."

"Use it, you'll lose it," said Brian.

"Can you get your arms around that?" asked Alison.

"Aw, c'mon, guys," said Vandal, "I'm just trying to light a fire under this weenie." He shook his head in disgust, jammed the lighter back into a pocket of his jacket and spat out the cigarette. He winked at Mara and sneered at me before he stomped away.

Spike swung around and led the Mutant Pack back into the rec room.

Mara and I didn't have much more to say. I walked her to the elevator. I just wanted to get back into bed.

"Well, uh, have fun," I said.

"You, too." She realized that didn't make much sense. "I mean . . . I'll see you." The elevator door opened and she was gone. I didn't expect to see her again. I wasn't sure if I felt sad or relieved.

"Get off my back," said Vandal. "I'm under stress."

"Poor baby's got cancer," said Spike sarcastically.

"You disrespected Fred in front of his lady," said

Brian. "That is not cool."

"I went a little chemo crazy."

"Can you go crazy from chemo?" I asked.

Dr. Wallabini cleared his throat. I couldn't see his mouth because of all the medical journals on his desk. "The literature shows evidence of episodes in which patients may have hallucinations or delusions, but . . . "

"See," said Vandal. "I'm on a new experimental protocol, the stuff makes me a little nuts. Listen, Frad, next time your babe comes, I'll let you make me look bad, okay?"

"That'll be easy," snapped Spike.

"Chemo crazy," said Alison, almost dreamily. "Will each of us go crazy in our own special way?"

"According to the literature," said Dr. Wallabini, "one tends to act out in accordance with one's basic personality."

"Got it," said Brian, looking at Vandal. "Jerks act out like super jerks."

"And wimps will always be wimps," said Vandal, looking at me.

"What's your problem with him?" asked Spike.

"He's a lump with a lump," said Vandal. "He's not out there slugging. He doesn't even have a visualization yet."

Everyone was looking at me. "Well, uh, Ranger. He goes around my body, and, uh . . ."

"Kills cancer cells," said Alison, helpfully.

"Well, uh . . . he doesn't actually kill . . ." Ranger

45

never killed anyone. I tried to think of what he could do. "He, like, collects them?"

"What a wimp," said Vandal.

"I think we've had enough for today," said Dr. Wallabini. "Now, don't forget. My door is always open."

That night I dreamed of The Game.

He was out of strength chips and he was out of luck, but he struggled till the end against the searing staples that clamped his wrists to the radioactive dump. Ranger never quit. But Ranger always died.

I woke up.

A clump of my hair was lying on the pillow. I shuffled into the bathroom.

In the mirror I saw a bald patch over my left ear. It was about six inches above the red surgical scar. I felt nauseous. Then I looked on my right side and saw the second lump.

Just below my right ear another egg was trying to break through the skin.

Mom and Dad watched Dr. Wallabini examine me. He made a big deal of pretending it was no big deal. "Don't panic. It happens."

"What will you do now?" squeaked Mom.

"We do not have a great deal of data on this type of cancer," said Dr. Wallabini, "so we will attack it in two different ways. One,"—he was ticking them off on his stubby little fingers—"we will increase

the dosage of chemotherapy. And two, we will begin an experimental hormone to increase Frad's
natural strength so that his own system can more
efficiently combat the cancer cells." He smiled and
waggled his fingers. "Frad will save himself."

Dad cleared his throat. "And that's worked in
other cases?"

Dr. Wallabini cleared his throat. "This is the first
time we have ever tried it."

8

DAD COULDN'T WAIT to show me the basement. "We'll work out together," he shouted as he pounded down the steps. "We'll get in superhuman strength."

I lurched after him on wobbly legs, grabbing the banister and walls for support.

"Don't be long," yelled Mom from the kitchen. "I'm making a great dinner. All Freddy's favorites. My greatest hits."

I wished they weren't so upbeat. It made me tired. They'd chattered the whole trip home from the hospital, what a good summer we'd have, trips, movies, dinners out.

48

It made me wonder if they knew something I didn't know. Was this my last summer?

"Some layout," said Dad proudly. "What do you think?"

I hated it. The cracked old leather couch was gone, the dusty computer, the curling CyberPunk poster, all gone. My cave was gone.

In its place was a health club.

On the wall-to-wall green carpet stood an exercycle, a rowing machine, a weight-lifting bench with a rack for barbells, all facing a huge ceiling-to-floor mirror that stretched across one wall. So you could watch yourself turn superhuman.

"So what do you think?"

"Be great," I mumbled.

"Your mom thinks this is really for me, I'm just using you as an excuse." He grinned. "Always wanted a home gym. And a workout partner."

He stepped back to admire it. "Free weights give you more muscle flexibility. At least that's what the salesman said." He tapped the barbell on the rack. "Three hundred pounds on that sucker right now. We'll start you at twenty, work up slow. You'll be Schwarzenegger by spring." He pointed to the exercise machines all poised to charge into the mirror. "These babies are electronic. They can record your heartbeat, blood pressure, skin temp and caloric expenditure."

I tried to think of something positive to say. "Must have been pretty expensive."

"Hey." Dad's face got twisted. "There's no price on you getting well." He started to open his arms, as if he was going to hug me, then just shrugged. "Gotta call the store. Don't hurt yourself. Wait till I get back." His eyes were wet. He turned and pounded up the stairs. The noise hurt my head. Why couldn't he just walk up?

I wandered around the room, stroking the cool, silvery skins of the machines. I couldn't imagine myself on any of them. Especially with Dad. We never did much together. Not that we didn't want to, it just never worked out. He was always working so hard, first to save money for the store, then to keep the store going. For the last five years he had spent almost all of his time at Software Junction. Mom was working there most of the time, too.

We didn't do much in the way of family vacations or hanging out together on weekends. Mom and Dad tried to come to any event I was involved in, but I didn't give them a lot of major occasions. I was never the starting pitcher in a Little League game, never had a lead in a school play or gave a valedictory address or even was one of the mini ministers at Youth Sunday at our church.

I was the guy in the back row of the chorus, on the bench at Little League. I sang. I played. I was there. We think. I never sounded off-key or dropped a crucial fly ball, but I was never a reason to close down the store. No star, no hero. I never made much of a difference.

And now look at me.

The scar on the left side of my neck was a red mouth crisscrossed with black stitch marks, and the lump on the right side was marked with purple dots as targets for the radiation treatments. My hair was a pathetic garden of scraggly weeds. My face was beginning to puff out from one of the chemotherapy drugs. Coming attractions. I could make out a faint greenish tinge on my cheeks.

I imagined the head in the mirror, green and swollen and bald, and I began to cry. It was the first time I had cried since I was a little kid. I just sat down on the green wall-to-wall health-club carpet with all those silver machines and I sobbed and sobbed. I couldn't stop. It was like the vomiting. Long after all the tears were gone, I still had the dry heaves.

"It's okay, Freddy," said Mom. "Let it go, you'll feel better."

I saw them in the mirror, on either side of me, holding me.

"Sorry," I said.

"For what?" asked Dad.

"For all the trouble."

"It's not your fault," said Mom.

Not my fault. For being a wimp. For having cancer. For being a wimp with cancer.

I don't know where the days went, disappearing like pages scrolling up a computer screen. I woke

51

up late and moped around and watched game shows and took a nap and watched old sitcoms and had dinner and watched whatever was on and then I read and listened to the radio until almost dawn and then I fell asleep until it was time to wake up late and mope around some more.

After a while, Mom and Dad stopped trying to take me out to dinner and the movies and brought movies home from the video store. They were always slipping in movies about kids overcoming handicaps, learning to ski down the mountain on one leg, but I preferred the horror movies where a guy with a face like a pepperoni pizza wiped out the student council one cute preppie at a time.

I watched everything, thrillers, comedies, westerns, the classics with Humphrey Bogart and Alan Ladd and Charlton Heston. *The Maltese Falcon*. *Shane*. *Planet of the Apes*.

There was a movie called *To Catch a Thief* in which Cary Grant, to outwit the cops, wears a mask to a costume ball and makes sure everyone knows it's him. Then he gets a stand-in to dance all night wearing his mask while he goes out and nails the villain.

It made me think of the Halloween Dance. Maybe I would go disguised as a normal-looking kid.

I got a stomachache thinking about it. I had to get out of that date. First thing, when Mara comes home.

Mom took time off from working in the store to cook me nutritious meals and keep me company, but I avoided her, hiding out in the air-conditioned darkness of my room, under the covers. She tried to get me out on the deck, she said the fresh air would wake me up, the sunshine would make me feel better, but I felt naked in daylight, even balder, greener, puffier.

I never went down to the gym. Dad mentioned it at dinner once, but Mom shot him a warning look and he dropped it. "When you feel like it," he said. I didn't think he was using the machines either.

Whenever the phone rang I pretended to be asleep. I didn't want to talk to anybody. Mom said Jon and Jeff called a lot, and a few of the other kids from school. Jeff had a summer job on the weekly local newspaper, *The Nearmont Shopper*. Jon was working on the mainframe computers of an international corporation whose headquarters were in the next town.

Mara called a few times from pay phones on the highway near some woods where she was hiking with GreenAction. She sounded very concerned about me, she really cared. I told her about the experimental hormone, and that the second lump had stopped growing, which was good news. She told me to concentrate on getting well because we were going to be a great team when school started again. But her voice sounded so much stronger than I remembered it, even more self-confident, that somehow I felt weaker.

I lost weight, but I looked fatter because my face was so swollen. My eyes were disappearing. I started not to care, to feel numb, a computer turned on but not booted.

Dr. Wallabini looked at my blood test results and my X rays and said everything was fine. He seemed preoccupied, worried. When Mom started to ask him a question about my greening skin, he herded us out into the hall.

A nurse rushed up. "We're ready."

"See you next week." Dr. Wallabini followed her down the hall. Another nurse was pushing Vandal in a wheelchair. Vandal was clutching his elbows and he looked scared.

One morning Dad called from the store and asked me to bring over some invoices he'd left at home. It smelled like a setup to get me out of the house. I never would have gone if it was a warm, sunny day, but it was gray and cool for July. With a jacket and hat on I didn't feel so exposed.

Dad tried to get me to stay in the store and work for an hour or two, or at least have lunch with him, but I lied and said I was too tired and he let me go.

For a while, I sat in the car in the mall parking lot and watched people walk past. They were bouncing along, talking and laughing, and I felt as though they were living in a different world from me. I was from "C" City. I started to feel very sorry for myself. I was huddled into my jacket, my baseball cap pulled down over my face so no one would recognize me. As if anyone would recognize me now.

Suddenly there was a tapping on the windshield. A police officer was peering in at me. It was that grouchy Sergeant Durie.

"What's your problem?" he asked gruffly.

"Nothing, sir." But I thought, What's your problem? Why are you hassling me?

I felt a weird sensation, little prickles over my body. Dots of ice. I imagined chemo bubbles in my bloodstream and shivered.

Sergeant Durie leaned closer. "What are you hanging around here for?"

I felt energy flow up my legs, into my chest and arms. I had to grip the steering wheel to keep my hands from shaking.

"THIS IS A FREE COUNTRY." My voice was so deep and strong, it bounced off the roof of the car and filled it like a stereo blast.

Sergeant Durie jerked backward, as if I had poked him. "Don't you talk to me like that, kid."

"Sorry." I lowered my voice, but it still came out rumbly, from the depths of my gut.

My senses seemed super-sharp. I noticed tiny purple capillaries, like side roads on a map, threading from Sergeant Durie's nose up his cheeks. I smelled coffee and cigarettes on his breath. I heard the tick of his wristwatch.

"You kids around here think you can do anything you want." He pointed across the mall at the Near-mont Diner. "I know what goes on around here. You watch your step. Now beat it."

He kept glaring as I drove away. For a moment I was scared. I'm in trouble with the police. For the first time in my life in any kind of trouble. Then I thought, He doesn't even know who I am. He's just a frustrated old grouch who picked on me because he can't catch Roger dealing out of the diner.

He reminded me of Bang, the cop who spent all his time chasing the CyberPunk Rovers, in vain.

It must have been thinking about Bang that brought me down to the basement. I don't know what I had in mind. I wasn't going to work out. Maybe I had some dim idea about looking at the CyberPunk Rovers stuff.

My skin was still tingling with ice dots, and my senses were still sharp. The hum of the electronic machines behind me was a tidal roar. I noticed tiny scratches on the glass of the mirror, smelled the chemicals in the indoor-outdoor carpet. Should I talk to Dr. Wallabini about this?

Be great, said the puffy, green, bald kid in the mirror. Show Bini what a weenie you are.

I said, Don't you talk to me like that, frogface.

Talk any way I want, Fraid-eeee.

Dozens, scores, hundreds of icy specks blinked, a thousand icy prickles. Power surged through my body. I said, Hit the road, toad.

He said, Whaddya gonna do, wimp? Your usual nothing?

I said, Get your arms around this.

I grabbed the barbell, the one with three hundred pounds of weight.

The kid in the mirror said, Hit me with your best shot, wimp.

Don't push me. I'm tired of being an empty Styrofoam burger box floating along the storm drains of life.

Froggy laughed. Tell me about the cold fire, hero.

My voice filled the basement, the house, all of Nearmont, a thunderous roar:

"SOMETIMES, YOU'VE JUST GOT TO BREAK SOMETHING."

I threw the barbell into his stupid face.

I watched it in slow motion. Smoothly, in one continuous fluid motion, I picked up the three hundred pounds and hurled it at the mirror.

The kid disappeared in an explosion of shattering glass.

The barbell smashed into the mirror, wiping away that ugly grin, and bounced back onto the carpet.

Suddenly, all the strength drained out of my body. I was weak and dizzy. I sat down in a pool of chunky glass. I was never so scared in my life.

It was great.

9

"**S**o, what's the story?" asked Jeff. He was stretched out on the weight bench as if it was a tanning cot. What was left of the shattered wall mirror was crisscrossed with black tape. "The real story."

"Obviously," said Jon, in a bored tone, "he picked up a three-hundred-pound barbell and threw it at the mirror." He was pedaling the exercycle, monitoring his speed, pulse and caloric expenditure.

"I was there," I snapped. I was getting mad, at their attitude and at my mother for inviting them over without my permission.

"Just because you were there," said Jon, "doesn't mean you know what happened."

"I'm not crazy." As soon as I said it, I wondered if I was. Chemo crazy.

"No one said you were crazy," said Jeff in that nice, calm voice you use for crazy people.

"I'm not making it up," I shouted. I felt a prickle of ice.

Jon stopped pedaling. "What's wrong with your voice?"

"It gets deep when this power comes on."

Jon rolled his eyes and began pedaling faster and Jeff changed the subject, "So—you actually using any of this stuff?"

"Not yet."

"At least you finally got rid of all that Cyber-Junk," said Jeff.

"It used to embarrass me just to look at it," said Jon. "Three social defectives escaping their lives."

"What lives?" I asked. "We were in middle school."

"We should have been chasing girls, stealing cars, kicking butt," said Jeff. "Preparing for the real world."

"Role-playing games are a preparation," I said. "You learn decision making, values . . ."

"You learn to hide in the basement," said Jon.

"Moving right along," said Jeff. "So what really happened?"

"I told you. I felt this weird, cold feeling, like dots of ice all over my body, and I picked up the bar and threw it at the mirror." It was beginning to sound like something I had seen instead of lived. Like a movie. Or imagined. Like a CyberPunk Rovers adventure. "I had this surge of incredible strength."

"It doesn't compute," said Jon.

"You guys've lost it." I was getting annoyed. "At least when we played The Game you were into possibilities."

"Possible is a dreamer's word," said Jon. "Science deals in what's *probable.*"

"I got the strength from somewhere. What about all those hundred-pound women who pick up cars to save their babies?"

"Okay," said Jon. "Let's read that. We know that most humans operate at a fraction of their physical or mental capacities. Certain events can trigger a hormonal surge, adrenalin, what have you, and increase natural strength for a short time."

"If you could increase that fraction," said Jeff, "you'd have a monster. Star of the football team. Any girl you wanted. Scan a whole book in five minutes, get all As. Beat Roger and Tank into a wet smear. And all on a live syndicated TV show, the Bauer Power Hour." He cackled and wrote it down.

"If you could increase that fraction," said Jon, "you'd be in Nobel Prize territory. Not to mention patents worth billions."

"So you do think it's possible?" I asked.

"Negative," said Jon. "I think you had a hallucination. Massive doses of drugs can do that."

"What about the facts?" asked Jeff. "The weight

was moved. The mirror was broken."

"My theory," said Jon. "is the mirror had a flaw, an unseen crack. When Fred accidentally knocked the weight bench over, it set up a vibration that smashed the mirror. You should get your money back."

"You've been talking to my dad," I said.

"It computes," said Jon.

"On the other hand," said Jeff, "look at Spider-man, the Hulk, the Ninja Turtles."

"First of all," I said, "they all got extra strength from radiation. Second of all, those are comic-book characters."

"Isn't life a comic book?" said Jeff.

"Maybe your life," said Jon.

"Your life is a textbook," said Jeff.

"Okay," said Jon, "we've humored Freddy enough. Let's go to the movies."

"Three social defectives escaping their lives," I said.

"Not the same," said Jon. "There are girls at the movies. There were never girls down here."

I thought of Mara. "You know, there were never any major CyberPunk girl heroes."

"Scattergood," said Jeff. "That time we went after Dr. D. in New Budapest."

Jon dismounted. "You keep this up, I'm history. It's embarrassing."

"You won that one, Jon," said Jeff. "With an illegal strength chip."

"That is not true," said Jon. "You couldn't soft-head into the web, and Ranger stopped to save some kids. It was a clean win."

"You never won clean," I said.

"And you never won," said Jon. "Ranger always died."

Sudden silence. They studied the tape on the mirror. We'd avoided dealing with cancer or my baldness or my greenness, and now we were face to face with the real end of the real game.

Finally Jeff said, "The Game had no relation to real life."

"Wrong," I said. "If Scribe was alive today, he'd be spreading misinformation for big bucks on his own prime time talk show."

"C'mon, let's go," said Jon.

"Ace would be hacking into Exxon." I was getting into it. "He'd be spreading viruses and then charging corporations to disinfect their systems."

"Let's get some fresh air," said Jon. "Wake us up."

"Sunshine," said Jeff. "Make us feel better."

"You've been talking to my mom."

"She cares about you," said Jeff. "So do we. You can't stay cooped up in the house all the time."

"Don't worry," said Jon. "No one's going to make fun of you."

"That's smooth, Park," said Jeff sarcastically.

"He can't be a hermit," said Jon. "What's he going to do when school starts?"

It wasn't something I wanted to think about.

"By September," said Jon, "you'll look like E.T.'s older brother."

"That's very smooth," said Jeff, rolling his eyes.

"You might as well get people used to it now. So let's go."

"Thanks anyway. Some other time. I'm real tired."

Jon winked at Jeff and played his killer chip. "I got Alexander the Grape."

10

I NEVER COULD RESIST a ride in Jon's father's burgundy Jaguar. I lolled around the buttery tan leather backseat, my feet propped up on the console with the phone, the laptop computer and the fax. "How come he let you have it?" I asked.

"He's on a business trip," said Jon. "He sort of left the keys out."

He drove very cautiously through town. Jeff hung out of the front passenger window doing one of his live newscasts. "To you, it may look like just another suburban town, but for those who know and hate it, Nearmont is hell on earth. To our left, Dope Central."

Jeff pointed to the Nearmont Diner. Roger Sharkey's white BMW was parked out front between the twin blue 4x4s his twin goons drove.

I saw Roger's face framed in the window. I felt shivery. "There he is."

"Where?" asked Jon.

"In that middle window."

"Can't even see the window," said Jeff.

"He's eating french fries with ketchup," I said. How can I know?

"How can you know?" asked Jeff.

"I can smell it."

They laughed.

A police car glided alongside. Sergeant Durie looked us over. He seemed disappointed there was nothing he could pull us over for. He turned a corner.

"Now there's a guy on a crusade," said Jeff. "He's been calling my editor to do a story on dope dealing in Nearmont."

"Is he going to do it?" I asked.

"The editor says it's a bad image for the town. Besides, Durie's a little nuts on the subject. He's got this thing about Roger and the Mayor and kids these days."

I started to tell them about my run-in with Sergeant Durie in the parking lot, but we were circling the reservoir and the squat brown building behind the high chain-link fence.

What was going on in there?

I thought of Mara again. She'd decided to stay a

little longer at GreenAction camp. They had made her regional leader. She sounded very committed on the phone.

I wondered if GreenAction types sat around campfires at night, talking about barolium, planning actions, singing songs, getting close.

I must have been thinking about Mara for a long time, because we were three towns north of Nearmont when Jeff said, "I have this feeling we're being followed."

I looked out the rear window. My forearms tingled and the muscles swelled. I could see the faces of Roger's goons through the windshield of a blue 4x4 at least a half mile behind us.

"You see anything, Fred?" asked Jon.

Maybe I just imagined I did. I decided not to say anything.

"Road's clear for at least a half mile," I said, truthfully.

We ended up in a tenplex near the New York border and settled in for a few hours of car crashes, flying glass, bullet-riddled bodies and gallons of blood. The usual laughs.

But it wasn't much fun anymore. Every time fake blood splashed against the movie screen, real needles and veins flashed into my mind. By the time we staggered back out into the August evening, the furry fist of nausea was in my chest. I wasn't sure if I was feeling queasy from all the popcorn and soda or from the flashbacks of my own private movie.

"Uh-oh," said Jon.

Roger's goons were sitting on the hood of the Jag. They wore identical red jogging suits and headsets over their baseball caps. They clapped and shook to the music coming out of the portable CD players slung around their necks.

"They're scratching the finish," said Jon. "My dad'll kill me."

"Unless they kill us first," said Jeff.

"Either way I'm dead," said Jon.

"Be cool," said Jeff. "I'm right behind you."

They forgot about me and marched up to the car. I followed them, a thousand prickles on my back and chest. Power surged up my legs, out into my arms. My senses sharpened. Even in the dusk I could see the letters BARRY on one twin's gold neckchain, the letters LARRY on the other's. I smelled the beer on their breaths, heard the country and western on one CD player, the heavy metal on the other.

"My dad's car," said Jon. "Give me a break."

They slid off the hood of the car.

"I really appreciate that, guys," said Jon.

They surrounded me. They were huge. Barry grabbed my right arm, Larry my left. I wondered if they were going to finish the job Tank and Roger had started and pull me apart like a fried chicken.

"You don't want to risk this," said Jeff. "I just read in the current *New England Journal of Medicine* that you can catch cancer by beating a cancer patient."

"That's real stupid," said Larry. "Now beat it before you catch some of this." He made a fist.

Barry began pulling me toward the 4x4. "Roger needs to talk to you, Freddy. Clear up the Prom thing."

"He's really very upset," said Larry, "which makes us very, very upset."

"He says he needs to know where you're at," said Barry.

"I'm right here," I said, stopping. The power in my legs nailed me to the ground. "This is as far as I go."

They started pulling me, but they couldn't budge me. My arms felt like tree trunks. They looked at each other strangely.

"This is kidnapping," said Jon.

"Go call the police," said Larry. "I can scratch the number on your door."

"We'll follow right behind," said Jon.

"That's fine," said Barry.

My voice was an ice storm. "I'm not going anywhere with these dirt bags."

"He didn't mean that," said Jeff.

"Look," said Jon, "you guys can sit on the hood. You can sit inside, call Roger from the backseat, send him a fax even. Please leave Freddy alone."

"That's really nice, Jon." I felt touched. "But it's not necessary."

I flexed my biceps, squeezing Larry's and Barry's arms in the crooks of mine.

They howled in pain.

"Hit the road, toads," I roared, grabbing each of them by the seat of their pants and banging them together like cymbals. They fell down and tumbled over each other trying to get up.

I grabbed them by the front of their jogging suits.

"You tell Roger," I thundered, "that if he wants to see me, he better call for an appointment."

I let them go. They ran away.

I sat down hard on the asphalt, suddenly exhausted. The energy gurgled right out of my body.

"Are you okay?" Jeff helped me up.

"Now do you understand what I've been trying to tell you?" I gasped.

"No," said Jon. "Just because we were there, it doesn't mean we know what happened."

11

D R. WALLABINI WAVED me in through his open door, but he didn't stop tapping on his computer keyboard.

"I need to talk to you."

"My door is always open."

"Could we close it?"

"That gives the wrong message, Frad." He kept tapping. "Secrets lead to fears, fears to negativity. How are you feeling?"

I took a deep breath. I really wanted that door closed. "Dr. Wallabini, I know this sounds crazy, but I think I have superhuman powers."

"Excellent," murmured Dr. Wallabini.

"I threw a three-hundred-pound barbell."

"Outstanding."

"I beat up two goons."

"Positive attitude equals positive results." His eyes never left the computer screen.

"Dr. Wallabini, please listen to me."

"I am listening to every word." He finally looked up. "And more important, I am also hearing what you really mean." He swiveled in his chair and stood up. He wasn't that much taller standing. He came around the desk. "You threw the barbell as one throws off a malignant tumor. You beat up the goons as the chemo would destroy the cancer cells left in your body.

"Frad, you are doing very well because you have come to understand that the most powerful muscle in your body is your mind."

"You think it's all in my mind?"

"It is more complicated, of course." He poked a stubby finger at the piles of paper on his desk. "My research, my statistics are going to prove that the cutting edge of cancer treatment is in the patient's own imagination.

"Twenty years ago, when I first came into the field, the surgeon was king. Every doctor wanted to be a blade. And then radiation was big; everyone was a zapper. And then chemotherapy—the lab rats were in charge. Now, the challenge is to put all those approaches together in one cart pulled by the power of the mind. That's good." He tapped out something on his computer. Just like Jeff, I thought, always taking notes on himself.

"Do you think I made it all up? The barbell, the goons?"

His voice was patient and kindly. "As we enter more deeply into the world of imaging, the border between reality and fantasy blurs."

"No super powers?"

"You may very well be able to do things you never did before as you tap into strengths that are already within you." He walked back around his desk and sat down.

"I'm really confused, Dr. Wallabini."

"But you are getting better." He clapped his little hands. "Your blood tests look good, your lump might even be getting smaller. When do you come in again?"

"Next week's check-up."

"We'll talk some more." He was tapping away again. "My door is always open."

12

MARA CAME OFF THE BUS looking older, thinner. Her eyes seemed deeper and darker, and her hair was a tangle. She kissed me without really looking at me. I drove straight to the reservoir.

We sat without talking for a few minutes. I wanted to tell her about the barbell, about what had happened outside the tenplex, but I felt tongue-tied, as if we were starting all over again. And I was confused.

I pointed at the reservoir. Silvery moonlight rolled off the water and up the windshield in smoky curls. "We sat right here almost two months ago. After the Prom."

"We were two different people then." She sighed

and drummed on the steering wheel. The hollows in her cheeks held the spooky light and made her seem even more mysteriously beautiful. She seemed distant. A stranger. I couldn't believe I had taken her to the Prom. She said, "We've both had life-changing experiences."

I tried to steel myself. She was going to tell me she had fallen for a GreenAction guy. I could imagine Mara and this Greenie, one of those natural-food types, all lanky, rower's muscles, sneaking away from the campfire for a little GreenAction of their own. I turned up the volume on the tape deck.

She turned it down. "We've got to talk, Fred."

Sure we do. It's time to break the news to the frog she left behind. But she feels bad about it because this pathetic jerk went out and got himself cancer. "No big deal," I said coolly.

"It's the biggest deal there is."

I tried to remember how the hero did it in the old movies, letting her go without letting her know that his heart actually hurt. Bogart in *Casablanca*. I turned the ignition key. Maybe I should make up something about me and Alison.

"What are you doing?"

"Taking you home."

"I thought you were different. Cold fire. Hero is a person." Now she sounded hurt. What kind of a number was she running? "I thought you really meant it."

74

I was getting angry. "Look, I understand, no problem, okay?"

"I don't think you do." Her voice was sharp. "This planet has cancer, and if people like you and I don't do something together, there's no hope."

"Together?" I turned off the ignition.

"Freddy, there is so much we can do."

I said the first dumb thing that popped into my mind. "You won't believe this, but I thought you didn't want to see me anymore. You still want to go to the Halloween Dance?"

She shrugged. "I'm not as hardline as some of the Greenies. I think you can have a social life so long as it doesn't interfere with saving the planet."

"I'll get a wig if it bothers you."

"You're lucky—you've got a nicely shaped head." She stroked the wispy hair on my skull. "You should shave it all off."

I leaned back in the seat. I couldn't keep from smiling. "When school starts, I'll join the Ecology Club, of course."

"Kick those wimps into action."

"Sometimes you've just got to break something."

Through the smoky haze I could make out the high chain-link fence surrounding the squat building. "Find out what's going down in that place. Barolium."

"Baronium. We learned in camp it's been linked to certain types of new cancers. Maybe even what you got."

Suddenly, under my skin, I felt icy specks from my toes to my scalp. My senses sharpened. "Vegetarian pizza."

"Lunch at camp today. Our last meal. How did you know?"

"I can smell it."

"Sorry." She put her hand over her mouth. "I brushed after I ate."

"Mint toothpaste."

"How did you know that?"

"It's really weird." Across the reservoir, a container truck paused at the gate of the chain-link fence.

"Fred? You're shivering."

Energy surged up from my legs, flooded my body. I heard the gate swing open, metal scraping over gravel. I saw tiny lettering on the truck's cab. "Sinclair Ecosystems."

"Environmental gangsters," spat Mara. "How do you know about them?"

"It's on the truck." My voice was low and rumbly.

"What truck?"

"Pulling up to the plant."

She leaned her forehead against the windshield and squinted into the silvery soup. "I can barely see the plant."

I twisted the ignition key and kicked the car into life. I felt charged, electric, on the Edge. "Buckle up."

I spun out of the parking area and raced around

the reservoir. There had better be a truck there, or I was truly insane.

"I never saw the gate open before," said Mara.

I shut off my lights and pulled off the road. A corrugated iron door on a side of the squat, brown building had been rolled up so the container truck could back in. I focused my super senses. Foul chemicals tickled the hairs in my nostrils. I heard the clatter and boom of a machine, steady as a drumbeat.

"I think they're pumping something out of the building and into the truck."

"Toxic wastes." Her eyes were wide, her lips tight. "I've got to get in there. Might never get this chance again." She was rummaging in her pocketbook. A small flash camera. Plastic vials. "Hit the horn twice if someone comes to close the gate." She was out of the car, running in a crouch.

I watched her scurry through the gate and along the fence until she found a long shadow that covered her sprint to the building. I lost sight of her as she turned the corner.

I tracked her with other senses. Or was I hallucinating? Could I still be smelling the mint vegetarian pizza on her breath, could I really be hearing the crackle of her running shoes on the gravel path around the plant?

I'd never felt so many ice dots. They were everywhere, behind my knees, in my ears, between my toes.

A dog barked.

I imagined a guard dog foaming at the mouth, bursting out of a shadow to lunge at Mara's throat. Got to warn her. I threw open the door and started to leap out of the car before I felt the safety belt tighten across my chest and belly.

Jerk!

The dog barked again. I concentrated on the sound until I pinpointed it from a yard across the reservoir. False alarm.

Was I hearing things? Or really hearing things?

Human voices. A cheering crowd. Baseball on radio or TV. From inside the plant. The sound must be coming through an open window or door. Unless I can hear through concrete. Maybe I can see through concrete. X-ray vision. Into the girls' locker room.

Superjerk.

Thinking about the girls' locker room slowed my reaction to the distant burp of an electronic sensor that triggered the hum of an almost-silent alarm. The snick of metal rubbing metal. The gate was closing.

They must have spotted her. They were locking her in!

I hit the horn twice.

Her face floated in the darkness, a pale dime. Men shouted, booted feet crunched over the gravel. Mara disappeared. Floodlights clicked on, washing the grounds in daylight.

Concentrate.

I isolated her running steps, lighter, quicker than the others, moving along the fence. There were at least three other pairs of running feet. I smelled nachos and beer, diesel fumes, chemicals I couldn't identify. Baronium? The truck sputtered, started. Headlights dazzled me. The truck lurched out of the loading bay. The corrugated iron door whined down and slammed shut.

I slapped the car into gear and eased it back onto the road that curled around the outside of the fence. I followed Mara by her light running steps and the minty pizza. Got to stay close as I can, find some way to help her get out of there.

How?

Study the layout. The plant is in the middle of a small field surrounded by a twenty-foot chain-link fence topped by coils of razor wire. As long as the gate was closed, the only way out was over the fence, but the fence was too high to climb. Have to get back out through the gate. When the truck comes out.

But the truck was following Mara, grinding along behind her, reaching for her with its blazing headlights.

"Fred!"

She was trying to climb the fence. I drove alongside her, stopped short in a spray of stones. I remembered to snap the safety buckle before I leaped out.

When she saw me, she began pushing her camera and the plastic vials through the fence. "I can't get over this fence. Get these to GreenAction—they'll know what to do."

"What about you?" That deep powerful voice rumbling out of a body vibrating with energy was mine.

"I'll have to take my chances."

"I can't just leave you here."

"The planet comes first." She was so beautiful in the silvery light, her eyes charcoal, her hair wild, a brave scratch on her cheek.

The shouting came close. "There she is!" Crunching feet, the squawk of walkie-talkies, the distant scream of a siren. The container truck was bearing down on Mara, pinning her to the fence with its headlights. I grabbed the fence and pulled.

"Fred, what are you doing?"

The mighty voice roared, "*Just hang on.*"

I was an avalanche of ice, all power. My fingers were claws of steel and the fence posts groaned in their concrete wells as the strength that roared up my legs and back, through my shoulders and out my arms pulled down the fence. Mara scrambled up the bending fence. A light flashed in my eyes. Her camera had gone off.

I dragged the fence down on top of me and held it as Mara leaped over the razor wire. When she was safely on the ground beside me, I let go of the fence. It creaked and shuddered as it slowly returned to its upright position, just in time to block the truck and a half dozen men in brown uniforms.

We jumped into the car, and I burned rubber spinning out of the gravel shoulder. She clutched the vials and the camera to her chest, and we couldn't stop laughing until we were in a town miles away, on the other side of the county, ordering shakes and fries from a drive-up window.

"This is bad food," said Mara, "all chemicals and grease, and the packaging isn't biodegradable."

"Tonight, I think, Mother Nature will forgive us."

We started laughing again. By the time the food arrived, I was beginning to lose energy. Dots were melting all over my body. My arms and shoulders ached. My eyes burned, my ears rang.

"You okay?"

"Yeah." It was a struggle to keep my head up.

"That was so amazing. How did you do it?"

"I dunno." I was slurring my words, I was so tired. "Mine drivehome?"

I dozed on the way back. Mara woke me up on my street. There were police cars in my driveway.

13

I FELT SMALL AND WEAK and bloated and green. "What'll we do?" My voice squeaked.

Mara's voice was firm. "Whatever we have to do." She led me into the house. "Remember, we were in the right."

The living room swarmed with uniforms, blue Nearmont police, tan county sheriff's deputies, gray state troopers, brown private security guards.

"You okay?" boomed Dad. He barreled right through all those uniforms like a tight end, clearing a path for Mom. They hugged me.

"Where you been?" asked a trooper.

"Burger Shack," said Mara. "In Ridgevale."

"Long way for a hamburger," said a deputy, rolling her eyes.

"Shakes and fries," said Mara. "Could Freddy sit down? He's very tired."

"I'll bet you both are," growled one of the security guards. He wore a brown baseball cap with the words TOP GUN in gold. "We got your license plate number."

Dad led me to the couch and sat me down. "Maybe you'd rather go right to bed." He squeezed my arm. "You don't have to talk to these people." He looked happy.

"Be okay," I said. I felt good. Not even scared. Dad and Mom were on my side. And Mara and I were in the right.

"We've got questions," said a trooper.

"This is a county case," said a deputy. "We've got questions."

"Happened in my town," said Sergeant Durie. "We'll ask our questions first."

"First thing in the morning," said Dad. "Not now. Fred needs his rest."

"Pulling a fence down makes you real tired," said Top Gun.

"You pressing charges?" asked Sergeant Durie.

"Breaking and entering," said Top Gun.

"No locks forced, no doors or windows broken," said Sergeant Durie, looking at his little leatherbound notebook.

"The fence is bent," said Top Gun.

"Well, let's figure out who did that," said Dad sarcastically. "This hundred pound girl or this boy undergoing chemotherapy for cancer?"

The word punched a hole in the room and all the air whooshed out. The uniforms froze. I wished Dad hadn't used the magic word. I felt nauseous.

Sergeant Durie cleared his throat. "Let's just establish one thing here." He looked at me. His eyes narrowed. I wondered if he remembered my talking back to him in the parking lot of the mall. "Fred, were you on the grounds of the plant tonight?"

"No, sir," I said.

Sergeant Durie turned to Mara, but before he could say anything, one of the troopers said, "This is a state interrogation."

"We don't have to allow any interrogation without a lawyer present," said Dad.

"These kids are in real trouble," said Top Gun.

"This is ridiculous," said Mara. She paused dramatically until every eye was on her. Her voice was strong. "You should be investigating what's going on in that plant. We were coming back from parking by the reservoir—"

"Parking," said Mom. She looked pleased. "Oh, Freddy." Dad grinned. You could tell they were both so happy. A few hours ago they had this kid with cancer, now they've got this sexy guy who busts into toxic waste plants. What a comeback!

"—and we saw this huge container truck—"

"What truck?" Sergeant Durie flipped open his notebook.

The state trooper looked at the county deputy. "You check for tire tracks?"

"I thought this was *your* investigation," she snapped.

Sergeant Durie squinted at Top Gun. "What kind of truck on a Saturday night?"

"I'm not on trial here," said Top Gun.

"Nobody is," said Dad, smoothly. "Why don't you people sort all this out, and then come back. Fred and Mara aren't running off to Brazil. At least not tonight." He winked at us.

"Mr. Bauer," said Sergeant Durie, "I'm not sure you're taking this as seriously as it deserves. There may have been a crime committed here."

"There sure was," said Mara. "And I think he has the answers." She pointed at Top Gun. "Tell us about that truck."

Top Gun started for the door. "You folks are gonna have to deal with our lawyers."

"Wait a minute now," said Sergeant Durie, but Top Gun was out of the house

"That's taking charge, Durie," snickered the state trooper.

Sergeant Durie's face got red, but all he did was snap his notebook shut. The uniforms milled around the living room for a few more minutes and talked among themselves and to Dad, but my brain had slipped into a puddle in the back of my head and I couldn't follow the conversation. Mara sat next to me on the couch and squeezed my knee. I had trouble keeping her face in focus, but it looked beautiful.

"You were terrific," she whispered.

"Hey, fence busters." Dad loomed up, chuckling and rubbing his hands together. "Sure had a busy night."

Mara stood up. "I better get home. My bags are still in the car. I haven't seen my folks yet."

"I'll drive you," said Mom. "Don, you better get Freddy upstairs."

Mara kissed me on the cheek and followed Mom out as Dad pulled me up from the couch. "Let's go, big fella."

On the way up the stairs, I said, "Dad? Could we start lifting tomorrow?"

"Sure. What made you think of that?"

"I figure, if I can pull down a fence like that the way I am now, can you imagine what I could do if I was in shape?"

He laughed and put his arm around me as we climbed upstairs.

14

WOKE UP SORE ALL OVER. My body felt chipped and torn in places I had never heard from before. I couldn't get out of bed until late afternoon. Dad and Mom just kept grinning at me through dinner. Dad said the Mayor had stopped by the store to tell him there was nothing to worry about, no charges would be pressed. Sergeant Durie had overreacted, and he would be reprimanded.

It didn't make a lot of sense, blaming everything on grouchy old Durie, but I didn't think about it much. I was too busy listening to my groaning body and watching my head bump up against the ceiling again like a balloon.

Mara came by with a photograph of me pulling down the fence. The flash that had popped while she was climbing had frozen my face into a terrifying green gargoyle. You couldn't see what I was doing, but you could see iron cables standing out on my neck and cannonball muscles bulging through my shirt.

"I look like the Incredible Hulk."

I guess she had never read the comic or seen the TV show, because she said, "Oh, no, Freddy, you were wonderful." She kissed me. "You were a hero. You had the cold fire." A lot of the soreness in my back and shoulders disappeared.

I noticed she was wearing serious clothes and carrying a suitcase. "Where are you going?"

"Washington. GreenAction headquarters. I'm going to get the samples analyzed."

"How long will you be gone?"

"As long as it takes."

"Where are you going to stay?"

"With my cousin. She does graduate work at Georgetown. Why?" She was smiling. She knew why I had asked. I guess if a greenish guy can blush, then I was reddish green.

I thought about her all the next day.

That night during dinner, very casually, I said, "Feel like pumping a little iron, Dad?"

Mom and Dad glanced at each other and jumped up. She was saying, "I'll have a great dessert when you're finished," and Dad was steering me toward the basement stairs while I was still chewing on the last of my broccoli.

We didn't do much that first night. We tried all the machines, read over the manuals and Dad spotted me while I pressed fifty pounds on the bench and did a few biceps curls with the little dumbbells. It all hurt more than I let on, but I wasn't going to say anything. He looked too happy.

"You're going to beat this thing, Freddy. You've got a great spirit." It took me a moment to realize he was talking about cancer, not the weights. "That whole business at the reservoir, it really gave your mom and me a lift."

"I thought you'd be mad."

"Are you kidding?" He massaged my shoulders. "Boy's never been in any kind of trouble in his whole life deserves to raise some hell when things get tough."

"Sometimes you've got to break something."

"You said it." He grinned. "When that old crock of a cop came into the store and started asking me questions about you, I told him to go across the street to the Nearmont Diner and bust the drug peddlers, not some kid fighting to—" He caught himself before he said "survive" or "live," and then he went on. "A few hours later, the Mayor came by, told me not to worry about anything. If I wanted to expand the store, he'd take care of everything, talk to the town council for me, the bank, the guy who owns the mall."

"Why would the Mayor suddenly want to do all that?"

"I guess he wants to help out our family. He thinks you're a brave boy." He squeezed my arm. "So do I."

Dr. Wallabini studied the photograph. "This is very good, Frad." He leaned back in his swivel throne and looked pleased with himself.

"I pulled down an iron chain-link fence."

"Excellent. This is all part of the reinvention process. Your world has been destabilized by the disease. How does one stabilize? Get well, of course. But until you do, while everything is rocking and spinning"—his hands began to rock and spin—"you must reinvent yourself as a person in control. Spike has reinvented herself as a tough jock. Brian is megahip. Alison is in a spiritual mode. Vandal is an outlaw biker. And you . . ."

"A superhero." I felt a sprinkling of ice dots. I smelled the food trays coming up in the service elevators. Fish cakes.

"Very good." He peered closer at the photograph. "Looks like *The Incredible Hulk*—it used to be my favorite show. About a scientist, you know. Is this what your hero, uh"—he tapped his keyboard—"Ranger, looks like?"

"I don't know." I'd never thought about what Ranger looked like. Maybe like me, only bigger, stronger, older.

"Well . . . " He spread his stubby little hands.

"Your door is always open," I said, on the way out.

On the way home, Mom asked, "So what did you and Dr. Wallabini talk about?"

"My mind."

"That must have been a short discussion." She began laughing so hard tears came to her eyes and she had to slow down. "Just a little joke. Oh, Freddy, it's good to laugh once in a while."

Tank Ganz was waiting on our doorstep with a bouquet of flowers. He looked like an ape who had just torn up a garden.

Mom invited him in, but he said he had to get to captain's practice. The football team had started working out.

He thrust the flowers into my arms. "We want to dedicate the season to you, Fred. We're all pulling for you, Fred. You're an inspiration to the whole team, Fred." He sounded like he was reciting a speech.

"Wait a minute. I don't understand—"

"Here's all you have to understand," he growled. "First day of school, there's going to be a big rally to kick off the football season. Be there."

He lumbered off.

"That was so nice," said Mom.

"That was amazing," said Jeff later. We were sitting on machines in the basement. I was rowing,

Jon was cycling and Jeff was tanning. "Tank himself came. Alone. Something's up."

"I've been thinking about it," I said, which was an understatement. "It all goes back to the Prom. Roger and Tank are still afraid I'll say something about the steroids, and the Mayor's trying to make points with my dad."

"The police found tire tracks along the fence," said Jeff. "The official explanation is that the truck hit the fence and bent it."

"Now that reads," said Jon.

"It's a cover-up," said Jeff. "The Mayor called my editor and asked him to forget the whole thing. For the good of the town."

"For the good of the town?" I asked.

"He said it would look bad, you know, image, real estate values?"

"It would *be* bad if the drinking water's poisoned," I said.

"You sound like Mara," said Jon.

"She should be here soon," I said. "Unless they ran her off the road or something."

"You sound as paranoid as Mara," said Jon.

"There's just too much weird stuff going on," I said. "It's starting to feel like the beginning of a CyberPunk Rovers game."

Jon braked. "Look, Freddy, let's not—"

"Take it easy," said Jeff. "The fact is that Tank and Roger and the Mayor all want Freddy on their side. Doesn't matter why. All that matters is how we can use that to our advantage."

"For what purpose?" asked Jon.

"To get girls, to take over the world, whatever," said Jeff.

I was glad when Mara came flying down the stairs. Her eyes were wild and her hair was a mess. "There were masking agents in the samples."

"What does that mean?" I asked.

"It means," said Jon, "that chemicals were added to make it impossible to get an accurate analysis of the water."

"Why would they use a masking agent unless they wanted to hide something?" I asked.

"Exactly," said Mara triumphantly. "I'm really encouraged. Jeff, you're a reporter—you can search the Town Hall files, find out who owns that plant." She sounded crisp and sure of herself.

Jeff sat up suddenly, as if the imaginary sun had gotten too hot. "Well, um, they might get suspicious."

"Then we'll be sure there's something going on. Jon, can you hack into the Sinclair Ecosystems network, find their Nearmont chemical reports?"

He nearly fell off the bike. "That's really, uh . . ."

"Sure they can do it," I said. "CyberPunk Rovers live on the Edge."

"Don't start that." Jon dismounted.

"True CyberPunk characters," said Jeff with exaggerated patience, "were in The Game for profit. So what's in it for us?"

"For you," said Mara, "a story you could sell to *Sixty Minutes*. For you"—she pointed to Jon—"a Westinghouse scholarship."

"Maybe," said Jeff, "we have our own scenario."

"What's that?" the rest of us asked together.

"There are two ways to change the world," said Jeff. I could tell he was making it up as he went along. "From the outside, always trying to pull down fences, or from the inside, where the power is."

"What are you talking about?" asked Mara.

"Look—the Mayor, Roger, now Tank, all want Fred on their side. This is our chance to get in with the big boys who really run this town."

"And become one of them?" asked Mara.

"No," said Jeff. "To make real changes."

"That never happens," said Mara. "People get inside and they become part of the problem."

"Maybe you don't really want to make changes," said Jeff. "Maybe you just want to make noise."

"Do you think that's true, Fred?" Mara was looking at me.

"Where do you want to be, Fred?" asked Jeff. "On the outside looking in, or on the inside pulling strings. That's good." He made notes.

"Fred?" asked Mara.

I felt like they each had one of my arms and were tugging. "Look," I said, "we're all on the same side here, so let's at least give it a try, work together."

Mara gave me a hard stare. Finally she said,

"Okay, Fred. I'm counting on you to keep these guys honest."

I looked at Jeff.

"You have my word," he said.

"His word is maybe," said Mara.

I looked at Jon.

"Science is honest," he said.

"It was a scientist who invented masking agents," said Mara. She checked her watch. "I've got to get home. I'm expecting a call."

"From GreenSleeves?" sneered Jeff.

"You don't know when to shut up, do you?" She stormed out.

Jon said, "She's right—you talk too much."

"Can't interrupt the flow." Jeff rubbed his hand. "When you're hot, you're hot, and I am on a roll. Frederick, Jonathan, prepare to be gods."

I had a sinking feeling in the pit of my stomach. For once I hoped it was nausea, not a premonition. "What's on your mind?"

"Relax, Freddy, the Wise One has a game plan. That rally is going to be the start of *our* season. There's a new show in town, the Bauer Power Hour."

15

I WAS WIDE AWAKE an hour before the alarm was set to buzz. I wasn't sure if I had slept at all. The long night was a flickering parade of numbers on the clock. My stomach had twitched with each click. In six hours, three hours, two hours, Fred Bauer, you remember him, don't you?—he was here, we think—will no longer be a forgettable face in the crowd.

But what will he be?

I'd always been nervous on the first day of school. You were supposed to be. Different teachers, some new kids, a fresh start. Another set of possibilities. But I'd never lost sleep over it before.

I'd never really expected anything special to happen. I felt safe and secure in my invisibility.

Now look at me.

The creature in the bathroom mirror was not a pretty sight. The stupid grin split a hairless green moon. My gums were puffy and purple. The whites of my eyes were yellow.

Mara was waiting for me in the seniors' parking lot. She was carrying a green tote bag and wearing a green baseball cap. They both had the Green-Action symbol, a tree with its leaves forming a fist.

Without a word, she plucked the Software Junction cap off my head and replaced it with a Green-Action cap. She looked red eyed and tense. I followed her into the school building.

It was early. A few teachers were standing around, drinking coffee and talking about their summer vacations. The Senior Greeters were practicing their smiles. No one paid us any attention.

"Hold this, Fred." She handed me the tote bag and began rearranging the main bulletin board to make room for the poster announcing the Ecology Club's first meeting of the year, a speak-out against Sinclair Ecosystems.

She seemed so sure of herself. Where does she get all that self-confidence? Why don't I have even a little bit of it? Why can't I always feel ice dots blinking on all over my body, power surging up my legs, my senses super-sharp, like I did the evening I chased the twin goons, the night I pulled down the iron fence?

If I really did those things.

"What's going on here?" Coach Burg swaggered up.

"Ecology Club meeting," mumbled Mara over her shoulder. She had push pins between her lips.

"Save your energy," chuckled Coach Burg. "No pun intended. Club's been canceled."

"Says who?" Mara almost swallowed the pins.

"School board. Budget cuts. Lack of funds." He noticed me. "Flip the lid. No caps inside the building unless you're varsity." He touched his own maroon cap with the white felt "N."

Mara spit the pins into her hand. "We are an official school club."

"Were. Past tense. Sorry."

"We can charge membership, raise our own money."

"Not on school property. Insurance." He swung around to me. "Hats off."

"You can't get away with this," said Mara.

"You deaf, boy?"

I took off the cap.

"It's you!" Coach Burg whipped off his own cap and placed it carefully on my head. "Honorary varsity, son. We're all pulling for you."

"This is censorship," howled Mara.

He ignored her. His eyes were damp. "See you at the rally this afternoon, Fred." He turned and hurried away.

"What rally?" asked Mara.

"Didn't I tell you?" I hadn't, of course.

Kids began streaming into school, calling to each other.

"Fred." Jeff grabbed my shoulder. "Where'd you get that cap?"

"He's one of *them* now," snapped Mara. She snatched her tote bag and marched away.

"What's her problem?"

"They canceled the Ecology Club."

"We'll get it back," said Jeff.

"We'll own the school," said Jon.

"What's happening?" I felt dizzy.

"The ultimate story," said Jeff. He pretended he was banging on my nonexistent shoulder pads. "You write it before it happens."

"What's up?"

"Just be ready at three o'clock," said Jon.

"I've got everything covered," said Jeff.

"We'll be with you every step of the way," said Jon.

Now I was worried.

Bells rang; the hallways were filled with kids moving quickly.

My homeroom teacher kissed me on the cheek, a first. All the girls smiled. Guys I'd never talked to in three years gave me little taps on the arm with their fists. Everybody noticed me. Everybody was nice.

I moved numbly through the day. Everyone nodded and made paths for me in the hall, left seats empty for me near the blackboard, made room for me at the lockers. Being noticed for being sick was worse than being ignored.

At lunch, Mara said, "Exactly what's going on?"

"Fred is going to try out for the football team today," said Jon.

"No way," I said. "According to the program, I'm just going to stand up there and let Tank dedicate the season to me."

"Jeff wrote the announcement," said Jon, "so you can disregard it."

"With your new powers," said Jeff, "you should be all-American."

Mara's face was getting red. "He could get hurt playing that stupid game."

"CyberPunk Rovers live on the Edge," said Jeff. "Besides when the star of the Nearmont football team calls for the reinstatement of the Ecology Club, people are going to listen."

"We were going to tell you all this at the last minute," said Jon, "so that you wouldn't tire yourself with unnecessary anxiety."

"You mean stop whatever stupid scheme you guys cooked up," said Mara.

"Jeff cooked it up," said Jon, "and it's not stupid. If it works."

"Can't miss," said Jeff.

"What is it?" I squeaked.

Jeff lowered his voice. "After Tank makes his little speech and hands you a signed football—"

"How do you know he'll do that?" I asked.

"I wrote the speech," said Jeff. "And took the ball around to be signed."

Mara said, "Fred, I don't think you want to get involved in—"

Jeff said, "I think you just want to *make* problems, Mara, not really solve them."

"I'm not going to sit here and listen—"

"Then stand up and leave," snapped Jon. "That seems to be your program."

Mara looked at me. "Should I leave?"

"No." I was being pulled apart again. "But let's hear them out."

"This is ridiculous," said Mara. She picked up her tray and books and marched away.

"She'll be back," said Jeff.

"What makes you so sure?" I started to go after her.

They pulled me back down into my chair. "When you're Mr. Saturday Afternoon, she'll come running like all the rest."

"What's the story, Jeff? For once, the truth."

"That's hurtful, Fred. Have I ever lied to you?"

"Just tell me or I won't go to the rally."

"If he tells you," said Jon, "you'll go. Promise?"

"Well, I'll . . ."

"Good," said Jeff. "Here's the plan. Utter simplicity itself. After Tank hands you the football, you will throw it into the stands, pick up Tank and hold him over your head."

"This is crazy—"

"It's elegantly simple," said Jon. "In front of everybody you will have demonstrated your powers. They will have to put you on the team. You will be a superstar."

"And beyond the mere game," said Jeff, "you will have reduced Tank to a toy and made yourself the king of the school."

"You guys are getting me into something—"

"This is very good," said Jeff. "Power Bauer is nervous, on edge, ready."

"Adrenaline and testosterone," said Jon. "Champ juice."

"You're all wrong," I said. "I'm numb. I don't feel a thing."

"This is good," said Jeff. "Power Bauer is cool. Confident. Ready."

"Hormones in check," said Jon. "The tiger's in the tank."

"You guys'll say anything." I said. "Ace and Scribe."

"Game time," said Jon.

"The Game's over," I said.

"Always time for one more," said Jeff.

"Ranger never quit," said Jon.

"But Ranger always died," I said.

16

I**T LOOKED AS THOUGH** the entire school had turned out for the football rally. Jeff and Jon steered me toward the field like cornermen for a champion fighter. I searched for Mara in the stands, but I couldn't spot her among hundreds of faces.

"Feel anything yet?" whispered Jeff. He started rubbing the back of my neck and shoulders with his free hand. His other one gripped my arm. Was he afraid I'd run away?

"Not yet."

"Not even a tingle?" asked Jon. He was gripping the other arm. Why are people always pushing or pulling me?

"Nothing."

"How are the old senses?"

"What's the opposite of super?" I asked.

"Inferior, substandard," said Jeff. "Rotten, lousy, second-rate . . ."

"Fred was making a point," snapped Jon, "not giving you an English quiz."

"Words convey precise meanings," said Jeff. "Only a computer nerd would—"

The rest of what he said was drowned out by the band. As we stepped onto the field, they broke into the theme from *Rocky*.

"Nice touch," said Jon.

"Thanks," said Jeff. "I leave nothing to chance."

The entire football team was assembled in the middle of the field. They were all wearing their numbered jerseys.

Their heads were shaved. And painted green.

"Stroke of genius," said Jon. "How come you didn't tell me?"

Jeff was trying to catch his breath. "Well, uh . . ."

"I guess this wasn't your idea," said Jon.

Jeff recovered. "Of course it was. I just wasn't sure they'd go for it."

"I don't feel a thing," I said. "Maybe my powers are gone."

"Just try," said Jeff. "We've got nothing to lose."

"*You've* got nothing to lose," I said.

"That's what makes it such an elegantly simple plan," said Jon.

On the fifty-yard line, Tank shook my hand. It felt like a meat loaf. "On behalf of the Nearmont High School Tigers, we're dedicating this season to you, Fred Bauer, a profile in courage."

"Hope you do better than last season," said Jeff.

"How'd you like to be dropkicked through the goalposts?" asked Tank.

"I don't think Fred Bauer would like that," said Jeff.

I felt nauseous, lightheaded, scared.

Coach Burg put his hand on my shoulder. "You've got guts, son. You're an inspiration to all of us. Now, let's get on with it."

Jeff and Jon stepped away from me. Jeff was taking notes. Jon was shooting cool looks at the cheerleader who had told him he resembled Elvis. I finally spotted Mara in the stands, looking stone-faced. I couldn't decide whether or not I was glad she was there.

Tank stepped forward with a football in his hand. "Every member of the team signed it for you, Fred. Now you throw out the first ball." He lowered his voice. "Just toss it to me, Fred. Then I give it back to you to keep."

He handed me the ball, took two steps backward and opened his hands. A drumroll, then the band fell silent. Not a single speck of ice in my body. I heard nothing special in the hush.

"You know what to do," said Jon.

I looked for Mara in the stands but couldn't find her.

Coach Burg blew his whistle.

"Just do it," said Jeff.

I remembered quarterbacks I'd seen on TV. I set my feet, drew back my arm, cocked the football behind my ear and let it fly, aiming for a spot beyond the stands a hundred yards away.

The ball traveled three feet, smack into Tank's forehead, and bounced back into my nose.

The laughter bubbled out of the stands long before I felt the blood trickle down my lips.

"It's okay," said Tank. He scooped up the ball and handed it to me. "No problem, Fred." He lowered his voice. "You just keep yourself alive till the end of the season and we'll win the state for you."

"Alive?" I croaked.

He squeezed my shoulders. "Pretending you're okay when you're terminal. It really whipped the fellas up. I wish the first game was this afternoon. We'd kick butt. Win before Fred's dead."

I grabbed him around the waist and tried to lift, but it was no use. No ice, no power, nothing.

Tank hugged me. "Winning is everything. If it takes a sob story about a kid with cancer or a few shots of 'roids, the real blue chips go for it."

"Let me go," I said. "I think I'm going to barf."

Tank jumped away and I ran off the field.

I dropped the football and I didn't look back, but I imagined hundreds of eyes, damp with laughter?—pity?—which is worse?—watching this round green thing wobbling across the cinder track and up the grassy hill and around the redbrick building.

Fool of the school. Got to keep moving, can't stop, just get out of here, never come back, where'll I go, how could I let this happen, never be invisible again, always be a joke, jerk.

I was rolling along the county road when a car pulled up alongside, a white BMW. A head bisected by a Magic Marker mustache popped through the sun-roof. "Yo, Fred." The car stopped in a spray of gravel.

"Hop in," ordered Roger Sharkey.

I was too weak to refuse. Just a Styrofoam burger box. I sank into the soft leather of the bucket seat.

"You are beautiful," said Roger, shifting with a shoulder roll, stomping the Beamer into speed. "You really. Stuck it to those lames."

"Stuck it?"

"You showed Fat Tank and the rest of those Neanderthals. What to do with their little football." Roger was shouting over the roar of the engine and the moan of the rushing wind. "You made the right choice, babes." He dropped a baggie in my lap. "Smoke one an hour before you get chemo. Cuts down on the nausea."

It was easier to stuff the joints into my pocket than argue. I felt too weak to think. Got to get to bed. Sleep. Maybe I'll wake up and it'll be all different.

"People think I have. No feelings, Fred. Just a cold dope dealer. How do you think I feel Tank gets all the awards because of my drugs? And he gets his doses for free. Because he makes everyone on the team pay top dollar for theirs. We have to work together, but Tank's no hero. In my book." He pulled up in front of my house. "Freddy. You need anything, anytime. Roger's your friend."

I stumbled out of the car. It roared away.

It seemed to take me forever to get the key out of my pocket and into the front-door lock. It took all my energy and attention. I don't remember hearing the second car pull up or footsteps on the walk.

I didn't hear anything until Sergeant Durie said, "You have the right to remain silent."

By that time, he was snapping on the handcuffs.

17

THE BACK OF THE POLICE CAR smelled of Chinese food, coffee, cigarettes and vomit. I gagged.

"You okay back there?"

"Just fine." I didn't mean to sound sarcastic.

"Don't get smart with me, kid." He sounded the siren to move two sports cars that had stopped in the middle of the road so the drivers could exchange tapes. "You kids think you can do anything you want, you own everything."

I should have felt afraid, handcuffed, arrested for possession, on my way to jail. But I didn't. How come? Was I already too dead to care?

What are they going to do to me, give me cancer?

Now that's CyberPunk. I laughed.

The police car bucked to a stop. Sergeant Durie twisted around. Through the metal grate his face looked like pink grapefruit sections. "Funny, huh?"

"I wasn't laughing at you."

"Better not. I've had enough." He stomped on the gas.

I tumbled around the back as the car screeched through town, taking turns on two wheels. When we got to the police station, Sergeant Durie jumped out, yanked open the back door and dragged me out.

He was muttering to himself. "Town's out of control. Got to start somewhere."

"With me?"

"With Roger Sharkey. If kids like you just said no, there'd be no drug problem."

I'd been inside the police station only once before, years ago to register my bike. I remembered a big old room with jolly old cops and battered wooden desks. Now everything was glass and chrome. A bored-looking woman in uniform sat in front of a starship console of computer monitors, radios, telephones. There was a closed office door marked CHIEF. I thought of Dr. Wallabini's open door. You always get one free call when you're busted. Should I call him? You're right, Bini, it's all in my head.

"Siddown." Sergeant Durie pushed me into a red plastic chair alongside a metal desk. He turned on a tape recorder. "Okay, from the top. Where'd you make the buy, how much, how long you've been scoring off Sharkey?"

"He gave me a present."

Sergeant Durie laughed through his nose. "And then he drove you home from school."

"That's right."

"Give yourself a break, kid."

"It's the truth." I felt chilled. Air conditioning? But Sergeant Durie was sweating.

"I'm ready to cut a deal, Fred. You give up Roger Sharkey, you walk."

"Even if I lie to you?" The ice dots were blinking on. Between my toes. Behind my ears. Why now? Why not on the football field?

"You give me a statement, how you bought and paid for those joints, that's all I need to get a warrant, search his house and car, pick him up, nail him once and for all."

A deep, rumbly voice said, "But it wouldn't be right for me to lie."

"What do you know about right and wrong?" Sergeant Durie's eyes were wild; he was foaming at the mouth. "Suburban brat born with a Nintendo stick in one hand and a charge card in the other, you're going to do what needs to be done."

"I'm not going to lie." I watched the sweat bubble up in the creases of Sergeant Durie's forehead. "Roger picked me up. He gave me the dope for my chemo." The energy flowing up from my legs pushed me up.

111

"Where you think you're going?"

"Make a call."

"When I say so." He pushed me down.

I don't know why I thought of Ranger, but I did. Ranger stapled to the radioactive dump, Ranger powerless and dying, and I stood up again and spread my hands and broke the handcuffs.

They snapped like worn-out rubber bands.

I didn't do it purposely, I don't think. I was just pulling my hands apart and the power flowed into my arms and hands.

Now I was scared. Would he draw his gun? Would I have to use my powers on a police officer?

"Oh." Sergeant Durie moaned. "Nothing works in this town." He looked close to tears. "What's the use?" He slumped into his chair. He buried his face in his hands.

He looked so sad, I almost reached out to pat his shoulder, but Mayor Sharkey burst in, followed by the police chief. "Fred! Thank goodness you're all right. I'll take you home."

On the way out, the policewoman unlocked the cuffs and took them off. She looked puzzled. The Mayor kept slapping me on the back. I could see the chief leading Sergeant Durie into his office.

"Poor soul just cracked," said Mayor Sharkey as he led me out to his creamy white Mercedes. "Couldn't deal with a changing world."

"What happened?"

"No simple solutions, Freddy. No black and white.

112

Life is gray, with colorful accessories." He laughed. "People who talk about right and wrong haven't been out there, on the edge, fighting for survival."

"Right is what works," I said.

He missed the sarcasm. "You're a smart boy. And we're all proud of you, hanging in there, giving us all a profile in courage. I want you to put all this behind you so you can concentrate on getting well. Pretend all this didn't happen."

"What happened?"

"That's it. Nothing." The Mayor drove with one hand. We passed the reservoir. "See that building?" He pointed toward the squat brown plant. "Some shortsighted, narrow-minded, pointy-headed people merely see an ugly little processing plant. But I see the future of Nearmont. Follow me?"

"What does it process?"

"Money, Freddy. This town needs police, firefighters, garbage collectors, health and welfare support services. Who's going to pay for it? Who?"

"Who?"

"Right again. That plant is going to pay for it, with its taxes."

"But what if it pollutes our drinking water?"

"Says who?" The Mayor looked mad. "A few nuts who love trees more than they love people?" He pulled into my driveway. "Thank goodness you're not one of them." He stopped the car. "You just worry about getting well, Fred. I wouldn't want anything bad to happen to such a fine young man."

"It's already happened," I said.

"I mean anything more, anything worse." He lowered his voice. I thought it sounded threatening. "I was able to save you from Durie this time. Who knows about next time? Some other nut case? And think about your father."

"My father?"

"Wouldn't want somebody wrecking his store, would you?"

"Why would anybody want to do that?" I felt confused.

"Why would anyone want to wreck that nice little processing plant? You follow my drift?"

I was afraid I did. It *was* a threat. But I didn't want to believe it. "No."

"You know the difference between a hero and a zero?" asked the Mayor, pushing me out of his car.

"No."

"One letter, Freddy. Don't make me mail it." He slammed the door and drove away.

18

I TOLD THE WHOLE STORY at shrink-rap, from the beginning, as if it were a CyberPunk Rovers adventure, no personal feelings, just action, from Mara finding the first lump at the Junior Prom through throwing the weights at the mirror and chasing the goon twins and pulling down the fence to Mayor Sharkey's warning.

I'd never had such an attentive audience before. I realized that I never really had an audience before, except when I was GameMaster. I liked their silence, the way their eyes were locked on me. Even Dr. Wallabini was paying attention. He stopped tapping. The only noise in the office was Vandal's raspy breathing. He had come in a wheelchair, a black tube hanging out of his nose. He had trouble keeping his head up.

Alison leaned toward me when I described the ice dots, the super senses, the energy that surged up from my legs; and Spike's eyes popped when I ran off the football field. When I snapped the handcuffs, Brian threw his fist in the air.

There were a couple of other kids in the office, but I didn't know their names. Fresh meat. They rolled their eyes at one another, but it didn't bother me. It felt good to let the whole story flow out.

I was listening, too. I had never gone through the whole story before, not even in my mind. It was as if, for the first time, I was seeing the entire journey laid out in front of me.

And it didn't compute.

When I was finished, they applauded.

"I think Freddy had an out-of-body experience," said Alison.

"What else could he have," asked Spike, "with that body?"

"I was wrong about you," said Brian. "I thought you were a brain-dead dweeb. You get the Oscar for visualization."

"You don't believe me?"

"Of course, we do," said Dr. Wallabini. "You worked very hard to create those images. They are uniquely yours."

"It was so beautiful." Alison wiped her eyes. "Oh,

116

Freddy, you really captured it, the hero within each of us struggling toward wellness. . . ."

"Bull!" Vandal coughed and sputtered and he spat out his words. "Real . . . chemo . . . power . . ." He began to choke on the black tube. I realized it went through his nose, down his throat and into his stomach. "Fred . . . you . . . can . . . *arrgghhh!*"

Dr. Wallabini punched a button on his telephone console and two nurses rushed in. "Better hook him back up, stat."

They wheeled Vandal out of the office, gagging and pulling at his tube.

"He will be fine," said Dr. Wallabini, but we all looked at each other as if we weren't so sure. "Now. We must have more to say about Frad's presentation, yes?"

No one did. I was a little disappointed. I would have liked to talk about it some more.

Finally, one of the no-name kids said, "What'd Vandal mean about chemo power?"

"The juice turns you loose." Brian laughed and high-fived Spike.

Dr. Wallabini cleared his throat and frowned his bushy eyebrows into a straight line across his brows. "In the literature, there are many cases of patients believing that the chemotherapy is doing more than destroying cells. It is part of the process by which patients gain control by reinventing themselves."

"He didn't snap those cuffs with his imagination," said Brian.

"Defective handcuffs," said Dr. Wallabini.

"The three-hundred-pound weight," said Spike.

"A flaw in the mirror," said Dr. Wallabini.

"The fence," said Alison.

"The truck hit it," said Dr. Wallabini.

"The twin goons," said Brian.

"Frad scared them," said Dr. Wallabini. "They sensed his determination, they knew he would never quit."

"He's on an experimental protocol, right?" said Spike. "Maybe the chemo's making him super—"

"That is science fiction, not science," said Dr. Wallabini. "Enough for today. My door is always open." He nodded as Spike led the way out. As I passed his desk, he said, "Give me a moment, Frad."

When everyone else was gone, he walked around his huge desk. His eyebrows came up to my chin.

"First of all, Frad, let me say how proud I am of you." He made a steeple of his hands, in front of his chest.

"You are?" That took me by surprise.

"From the beginning, you did everything we asked of you, you tried very hard, you were a good patient."

BUT. I could hear the but coming around the corner.

"But. Sometimes we try too hard. We lose perspective."

"I didn't make it up." I felt angry. Ice dots on my back and chest.

"I believe that, Frad." His voice was gentle. "That's why I am so concerned about you."

"I don't understand." I felt confused. The dots melted.

"Sit down." He waited until I was back in a chair before he walked around his desk to his swivel throne. "If you had made it up, if you were consciously creating a story to enhance your position among your peers, or to keep me off balance, or to keep up your spirits, I would be delighted. However, I am concerned because you have apparently internalized your reinvention to the point where you totally believe it."

"And that's bad?"

"It makes it that much more difficult to return to normal life. More important, it can lead you into emotional danger."

"I'm going crazy?"

Dr. Wallabini sighed. He looked like he really cared. I realized I sort of liked him. I couldn't be angry at him. And he could be right. "I would not use the word 'crazy,' because it has no medical meaning. But I would say that you are on the edge of a slippery slope."

He made the steeple again and tapped his fingers together. "You must be careful not to fall into the bottomless chasm of fantasy and lose your mind. And yet, you must not become too fearful to journey deep within yourself to find the strengths you didn't know you had."

"So what should I do?"

"Do the right thing." Dr. Wallabini smiled. "I'm so glad you understand. And now"—he gestured toward his computer—"my statistics call. Do not forget—"

"Your door is always open."

"And for you, Frad, my ear, too." He pointed to his phone. "I have left instructions with the nurses—if you need me you can even call me at home."

He thinks I'm so crazy, I thought as I left his office, that I need my own personal twenty-four-hour hotline.

I dreamed of The Game.

It was the biggest funeral in the history of the Chasm. But then, of course, no one had ever died before. The Mutant Pack carried Ranger's body on a giant floppy disc. They were all crying. Ace and Scribe and Scattergood followed the body. The dwarf medic, Splicer, was shaking his head. He could have saved Ranger if it had been only a matter of buying or stealing body parts. But the dork's sanity cells were gone, and those were irreplaceable. They buried Ranger in the basement.

I woke with an enormous headache. Iron flowers were blooming in my brain and pressing their

heavy metal petals against the inside of my skull.
My eyes were covered with sand. So was my
tongue. I sucked on ice cubes.

The phone rang.

"Fred?" The voice was so low I could barely hear
it. "C'mere."

"Who's this?"

"Vandal."

He was curled up in a corner of a bed in a private room. He was attached to so many tubes and
wires, he looked like a broken puppet collapsed under its strings. Machines hummed and beeped and
flashed numbers. The black tube in his nose snaked
into a machine on the wall. The machine gurgled.

"Yo, bro." He tried to sit up, but he was too
weak. He beckoned me closer. I dragged my chemo
rack and a chair to the side of his bed. "Don't . . .
listen . . . to Bini. . . . You . . . got . . . real powers."

"How do you know?"

"If we . . . get out . . . of this trap . . . alive—" He
gasped and closed his eyes. For a moment I
thought he was dead. I reached for the call button.
"We'll . . . ride . . . together."

"How do you know I've got real powers?"

"Wimps . . . like you . . . never . . . fake it."

He passed out.

121

19

THE FIRST FEW WEEKS of school no one could pass me in the hall without a grin, a wave, a friendly word. I got tired responding. Teachers kept assuring me I could take my time turning in papers, that I could schedule exams around chemo. Two different gym teachers offered to be my personal trainers. The librarian brought me books on beating cancer. I promised to read them.

My college advisor said that cancer might help me get into a better school. Colleges like interesting people in their student bodies, she said. Might be a slot in an Ivy for a kid who beat cancer. Maybe even financial aid. Of course, to qualify, you do have to beat it, she said.

And then, gradually, I began to fade away again. Tank and the football team lost interest in me after they lost their first game. They washed off the green paint and stopped shaving their skulls. I became the only person in school who looked like me. But everybody was used to it.

It's one thing to be invisible if you look like everybody else, but to be invisible when you're swollen and green and hairless is weird.

My friends weren't a lot of support. They had their own problems.

The school paper was shut down. Lack of funds, said the School Board. Coach Burg's revenge, said Jeff.

Then the Computer Team was disbanded. Lack of funds, said the School Board. Coach Burg's revenge, said Jon.

Jon and Jeff started having lunch with Mara every day. And listening to her.

Now, Mara kept asking, do you guys still believe in working from the inside?

The three of them would start whispering together. Mara always waved me into their conversations, but I pretended I needed to finish some homework or cram for a test. Once I even made believe I had to barf. Anything to avoid their plots and plans.

They saw everything as part of a giant conspiracy that involved Sinclair Ecosystems and the

Mayor and Coach Burg and Tank and Roger and the ozone layer and the Rain Forest and the networks and the multinational corporations. I didn't care whether they were right or not—I just wanted to be left alone.

Mara and I went out a few times, to movies and to listen to music, but her mind was locked on that ugly little brown building near the reservoir. I still liked her a lot, but I thought it was over between us.

Otherwise, I was having a pretty good year in school. And Dad and I were working out almost every other weekday night, and twice on the weekend. He was coming home earlier from the store. It was nice. Maybe there was an upside to cancer. Maybe I'd get something out of it after all. Like a college scholarship. That could help out Mom and Dad.

There was still the chemo, but Dr. Wallabini said that my test results were looking good. The drugs were doing their job, especially the experimental hormone, he thought. The second lump was shrinking. When it was gone, said Dr. Wallabini, he would end the chemotherapy treatments. My hair would start growing back, the puffiness would disappear, the green would fade. I couldn't wait.

Except for shrink-rap, we didn't talk too much during my October infusion. The World Series was on, the football season was in full swing, and the new TV shows had begun, so we logged a lot of tube time. Alison had some bad test results and spent a lot of time alone, on the telephone. Brian wasn't around—he was on a different schedule that month.

But Spike had just gotten her prosthesis, and she marched in and out of everyone's room showing the moves that had made her an all-state volleyball player. Her parents brought a ball to the hospital, and she slept with it.

Vandal was feeling better, which I was glad about until he was moved out of his private room and in with me. I figured a lot of noise and maybe even a fight. I wasn't going to take any stuff from him, I decided.

But he turned out to be okay. He didn't talk much. At least two members of his family showed up every day, and they were nice. They were always offering me the cookies and salami that he couldn't swallow either, and the cold noodles that we pigged out on because they went down so easy.

His family called him Vincent, which seemed to embarrass him when other people heard it. It helped me see him a little more clearly. Vandal was his fantasy name.

I had a strange dream one night. Ranger was stapled to the dump, burning to death as usual, but he was having a dream. While I was dreaming of Ranger, Ranger was dreaming of me.

They finally trapped Freddy in the Chasm, branded him nuts and whacked him with enough juice to staple him to the bed. Roger and Tank, Coach Burg and the mayor were laughing as the kid fried. Next time

I'll invent a hero instead of a zero, a kick-butt char-
acter who'll clean up the town. For starters.

"You okay?" Vandal was shaking me awake.

"Whatsa matter?"

"Man, you were rolling around, moaning, 'Ranger, don't die.'"

"Just a dream."

"Sounded like he was in deep, man." He sat down on the edge of my bed, leaning on his chemo rack. The tube was out of his nose, but his voice was still scratchy. "So what's the deal on Ranger?"

It was the middle of the night, so quiet I could hear the squeak of the nurses' rubber-soled shoes and the humming of equipment. I felt lonely and sad, and I trusted him.

"Ranger was a character in a game I used to play. CyberPunk Rovers?"

"I heard of that. Like a war game? "

That was all it took. It was a weak moment. A wimpy moment. I told him about Ranger and play-ing The Game with Jeff and Jon, and how I felt about Mara, about getting caught between Tank and Roger and being Mr. Nobody until I got cancer, all the personal details I'd left out when I talked at shrink rap. It was dawn when I stopped babbling.

When I was finished, he sat by my bed for a long time, and he looked sort of dreamy, even after the nurses bustled in—"Sharp stick!"—and took our blood counts, and the nurses' aides started moving things with a clatter and the hospital woke up around us.

Finally, he said, "So that's where you got all your ideas about your power. From the game."

"I thought you said you believed me."

"I do. But like everybody's got their own story."

"That's all I've got. I'm a wimp."

"Right. That's why I believed you. A wimp wouldn't make up something like that—he'd be too wimpy."

"You still think I'm a wimp?"

"Once a wimp, always a wimp." Somehow, the way he said it, I couldn't feel offended. "But now you're a wimp with superhuman power."

"Which doesn't always work."

"It always works when you think you're in the right. Right makes might."

"I don't get it."

"The ice dots come on only when you think you're right. Right? The twins. The fence. The handcuffs. It like triggers the juice. When you think you're wrong, like that football thing, nothing happens."

I got it. "Ranger could only do the right thing."

"But just having power is nothing unless you use it."

"You've got to break something," I said.

"Yeah. Raise hell. I always wanted to do that."

"You got your gang."

"You believed that?" He looked at me sideways.

I wasn't sure what to say, so I told the truth. "I did."

"Thanks." He closed his eyes. "Always dreamed of living on the Edge. Being somebody. Doing something that made a difference. Weird how getting sick gives you the chance."

"Chance for what?"

"We're gonna go to your school and close down Roger and Tank."

"We?"

"I hate 'em, Freddy." His eyes were shining. "You and me gotta take drugs to live. But they're pushing the poison to make money, to pump up their muscles for football. Vandal's got the handle. I'm mad. Those humps are history."

"History?"

"After that, you and the babe can go after toxic dumpers, whatever. I knew she was hot when I saw her."

"Be great," I said. He was into my fantasy.

"I'm feeling better just thinking about it." He looked better. "I'm gonna come along on your next run."

"Sure," I said, humoring him. "Vandal and Ranger, the dynamic duo."

Vandal shook his head. "Vandal's a good name, but Ranger sounds like a dog on an after-school special."

"Got something better?" I sounded annoyed.

"No offense. How about Cell Smasher?"

"Sounds like a cartoon."

"Captain Cancer?"

"Sounds like he spreads it."

128

He thought for a long time. "You get your powers from chemo, right? Something in it hits you a special way, brings out all the super powers we all got but can't get loose, right?"

"I guess that's about it. So?"

"So get your arms around your new name, Freddy." When he said it, I knew it was right and chills went up my spine. "The Chemo Kid."

20

FINALLY WENT DOWN and played The Game, for the first time in years. By myself.

I was supposed to be catching up on schoolwork. It was a Saturday morning, my first day home after the October infusion. Mom and Dad were at the store; the house was quiet. But I couldn't concentrate. Too tired. My throat and stomach hurt. And something kept calling me downstairs.

I didn't think about what I was doing. First, I dragged the exercycle and the rowing machine into corners. I left the weight bench in the middle of the room.

It took more than an hour to pull all the boxes

out of the bottom of the cedar closet and empty them on the indoor-outdoor carpet. The health club was becoming my cave again.

I set the computer on the weight bench so I could face it straddled on the padded board. I piled all the handbooks and notepads and discs on the floor around the bench. I hooked up the computer.

The last thing I did was tape the raggedy old CyberPunk Rovers poster to the mirror. One of the console cowboy's bionic eyes was torn. He seemed to be winking at me. Boot into the web, Ranger. Go for it.

WELCOME TO CYBERPUNK ROVERS
IF YOU DARE TO JOURNEY ON THE EDGE
CLICK ON

I clicked through the early stuff. I knew most of it by heart.

YOU ARE ENTERING THE WORLD AROUND THE CORNER—THE NEAR FUTURE, WHERE THE RICH HUDDLE IN THEIR ISO-BUBBLES AND THE POOR SCROUNGE IN THEIR SQUATS AND THE ONLY FREE CREATURES ARE THE CYBERPUNK ROVERS WHO LIVE ON THE EDGE WHERE EVERYTHING'S FOR SALE, ESPECIALLY INFORMATION, THE LIFEBLOOD OF THE NEW SOCIETY WHERE RIGHT AND WRONG HAVE BEEN REPLACED BY WHAT WORKS AND WHAT DIES.

I'd read that a hundred times, but it registered for the first time. Ranger always lost, always died,

131

because he never got it. He was still operating in the old ways, where right and wrong did count.

I punched in an old adventure I had saved, a good one, the last journey we'd ever completed.

I'd been GameMaster, as usual, and I had scrolled up a journey to New Budapest, the capital of the North. The Rovers' job was to arrange the defection of an energy scientist who worked for a corporation run by the Stilyagi, the Russian gang that replaced the Mafia and the Yakuza as world criminal powers. The scientist—we named him Dr. D. after a teacher we liked—had developed a new form of solar power that would not only run the world's machines but also reverse global warming. And it would give the balance of world power to whichever side had it, the North or the South.

It was a great game. Jon and Jeff and I had spent weeks in it. Every day after ninth grade, weekends, crouched around the computer in the basement, Jeff pacing, shouting, waving his arms, Jon arching his eyebrows, curling his lip, looking cool, old Freddy keeping them from killing each other, running upstairs for soda and cookies and chips.

It was our final journey, the adventure where it all came apart.

According to the rules, we could work together on the journey to New Budapest. We could operate as a team to spring Dr. D. from the Stilyagi fortress and make our escape out of the North. But once we crossed the Chasm, the free zone between North and South, it was every character for himself. Only one of us could claim the one-hundred-ducat reward for delivering Dr. D. to the Uhuru Corporation in Nairobi, Kenya, capital of the South.

Characters would kill for a hundred ducats. It was enough to buy a complete physical overhaul, including new eyes and enhanced immunity to disease; a new identity; and a year in the Pleasuredome.

We'd been fine on the trip north. Ranger was the strongest, so I took the hits when pirates ambushed us; and Scribe had the most money, so Jeff bribed the border guards and paid Splicer to replace my left arm when it was blown off in a firefight. Ace had the most info chips, so Jon jacked into other networks to work through the maze that got us into the underground bunker where Dr. D. was hidden, and out again.

We were only a few miles from the Chasm when the argument began.

Thinking about it, almost three years later, I felt sad.

Ace was driving the Land Rover. Scribe had the maps and Ranger was in back with Dr. D. When the overturned schoolbus appeared on the screen, Scribe said, "Keep driving," and Ace said, "No kidding," and Ranger said, "Stop. We've got to help them."

"We're being followed," said Scribe. "Stilyagi in pursuit."

133

Bleeding kids came up on the screen. Scattergood was with them. She had been driving them to safety after their homeless shelter had been bombed in a provincial civil war. The cursor arrow that represented our Land Rover started clicking past them.

"Can't just leave them there," said Ranger.

"Wanna bet?" said Ace.

"One hundred ducats says keep going," said Scribe.

"That's two against one," said Ace.

"Let's hire Splicer to help them," said Ranger.

"I'll need my credits for the border guards," said Scribe.

"Signal the Mutant Pack," said Ranger.

"Never know which side those crazies are on," said Ace.

"Call Bang," said Ranger.

"That's an official channel," said Scribe. "The Stilyagi'll be monitoring that—it'll give our position away."

"Those kids'll die," said Ranger.

"It's a world of risk," said Scribe. "We all live on the Edge."

"Do no harm for profit," said Ranger. "Protect the needy. Always choose right over wrong."

"There is no right or wrong," said Ace. "There's only what works and what dies."

"Let me out," said Ranger.

"Not till we get to the Chasm," said Scribe.

"Let me out now," said Ranger, "or I'll use my last strength chip to stop this vehicle."

"Then none of us wins," said Ace.

"What right do you have to do that?" asked Scribe.

"It's the right thing," said Ranger.

"Says you," said Scribe.

"This is stupid," said Ace. His voice changed. Jon said, "I quit."

"Do what you want," I said, "but we have to do something for those kids."

"Why?" asked Jeff. "This is only a game. We're characters. We're trying to win."

I said, "My character doesn't win like that."

"But why spoil it for us?" Jon stood up. "You screw up this adventure, Fred, I'm out of here. I'm getting tired of this stupid game anyway."

I should have said, Hit the road, toad. I should have stood up right there and shown some cold fire. But I was so afraid that The Game would end that I didn't do anything.

Typical Fred Bauer. He was here. We think.

Ranger couldn't leave those bleeding kids in the road. It wasn't right. It wasn't in his character. He was a real hero.

But Fred Bauer couldn't activate Ranger's last strength chip to stop the car, because he was a real zero.

Jeff said, "Jon, give me two clicks, okay?" He hit the keyboard. He blocked the screen with his body.

"Just as I figured," said Scribe. *"Those aren't injured kids—they're a holograph, a Stilyagi trap. Let's click out of here."*

135

We never did find out if that was the straight story or just another Scribe Report. Jeff clicked us through two screens into a mountain pass overlooking the Chasm, where it was every character for himself.

I tried to remember who won that last game, Ace or Scribe. I know it wasn't Ranger. They left him in the Chasm to die.

He never had a chance to escape because we never played another full-scale adventure. We hacked around some more, even started a journey or two, but that was pretty much it for The Game.

I thought about Ranger, stapled to the dump for eternity. Just like me. Even if I beat this cancer, even if someday I'm not fat and bald and green, I'll still be Fred Bauer, someone who's just here, not someone who makes things happen, a hero.

"So this is where you guys hung out." A female voice. Scattergood?

"It was a great time," said Scribe.

"We learned a lot," said Ace.

"Decision making, morality, character," said Scribe.

"What's really important," said Ace.

They were standing in front of me, Scribe and Ace and Scattergood. They were smiling. They had come back to save Ranger.

"What's really important?" asked Scattergood.

"Doing the right thing," said Ace.

"Leaving the world a little better than when you found it," said Scribe.

I was going crazy. Reality and fantasy had finally merged.

"You ready to play for real?" asked Scattergood.
Scribe said, "We need a GameMaster."
"We're clicking into Nearmont," said Ace.

It took me a long time to realize that the three of them were behind me, reflected in the mirror.

Mara and Jeff and Jon.

I felt hot and cold. I wanted to laugh and cry. All I could think to say was "What's going on?"

"It's a CyberPunk world up there," said Mara.

"We're going to fight back," said Jeff.

"We need your help," said Jon.

"To make a plan," said Jeff.

"We're going after Sinclair Ecosystems," said Jon.

"Sometimes," said Mara, "you just have to break something."

"We've got to flush them out," said Jeff. "I'm going to spread false stories."

"I'm going to inject a virus into their computer system," said Jon.

"I'm going to blow up their pipeline," said Mara.

"That's wrong," I said.

"What's right?" asked Jeff. "Shutting down the paper, canceling the Computer Team?"

"Poisoning our water supply?" asked Mara.

"If there's a right way," said Jeff, "then you show it to us."

"Be the GameMaster again," said Jon.

"I think I might be going crazy," I said.

"That doesn't mean you can't help us make a plan," said Jeff.

"Are you a hero or a Styrofoam box?" asked Mara. "Didn't you believe what you said?"

"It wasn't really me," I said. "It was from the CyberPunk Rovers Playbook." I started rummaging through the handbooks and catalogues at my feet.

"There's a lot of stuff in there," said Jeff. "But that's what you chose. What you remembered."

"Cold fire," said Mara.

I felt a sprinkling of ice dots. "We'd have to do it the right way."

"You've got a plan?" asked Jeff.

Energy surged into my body. I stood up. "No shady deals, no cutting corners. No lies, no viruses, no blowing up pipes." My voice rumbled.

Jeff stuck out his hand. As I shook it, Jon and Mara put their hands on top of ours. I felt my energy flowing into them and theirs into me.

"Ranger never quits," said Jeff.

"But Ranger always dies," I said.

"But Ranger always comes back," said Jon.

"This is no job for Ranger," I said. "He was a fantasy character in a kid's game. This is for real. This is a job for the Chemo Kid."

21

VANDAL PULLED IN first, roaring up on a monster black motorcycle I heard two blocks away. By the time I got out to the driveway, the neighbors were peeking through their front windows. I was glad Mom and Dad were still at the store. Vandal would be hard to explain, dressed in black leather with a skull and crossbones on the back of his jacket.

"Welcome to Nearmont," I said.

"You're welcome to Nearmont," he growled. "The 'burbs are for the birds."

When he started to lock his motorcycle, I said, "You don't have to bother out here."

"You kidding? Guys in trucks cruise for weeks to

rip off a bike like this one. How you think I got this baby?" While he locked it, I noticed that the crossed bones looked more like hypodermic syringes.

"Those supposed to be needles?"

"You're pretty sharp." He pulled off his helmet and grinned. His face was still thin and yellowish, and there were only a few wispy strands of hair on his scalp, but his eyes were bright and clear. "When you ride with the Chemo Kid, you got to be ready to stick it to 'em. You like that?"

"Vandal's got the handle." We shook hands, straight, power, jive and overhead. The Game had begun.

We were still in the driveway when the rest of the Mutant Pack arrived in Spike's van. Alison gave me a hug and Spike danced around me. "Which leg's plastic?"

Brian strolled coolly around Vandal's bike. "This antique on loan from some museum?"

Vandal snorted. "Tell that to a thousand Hell's Angels ready to ride up your tailpipe."

Spike jumped in between them. "When it's over you guys can fight, but right now the one who messes this up is gonna eat plastic." She cocked her right leg for a kick.

That's the Pack, I thought. They could save you, they could kill you, sometimes in the same adventure. The rowdy Mutants were always the wild cards in the deck. But they were the only cards I had.

They calmed down once we got to the basement.

Mara and I had set up tables and chairs and laid out soda, chips and a six-foot hero sandwich. We'd taped a giant map of Nearmont to the mirror, and a long strip of computer paper with the times of each phase of the operation.

"Some setup." Brian was inspecting the exercise machines. "You use this stuff?"

"I've been lifting pretty regularly."

"Let me feel," said Alison. While she squeezed my arm, Mara's nostrils flared. I liked that, all the times I'd felt little stabs of jealousy. "It's pretty hard."

"It's pretty hard to find," said Jeff, jogging downstairs. He stopped when he saw Vandal. "That your hog out there?"

"What do you know about hogs?"

"I know a bad bike when I see one, and that's a king hell classic."

"You're not as dumb as you look," said Vandal, pleased.

"That's not saying much," said Jon. His eyes clicked into Alison's. They both gulped.

I introduced them all around. I heard Alison say to Jon, "Has anyone ever said how much you resemble Elvis?" My first thought was, I hope this doesn't complicate the adventure. Romance can kill you. I was thinking like a GameMaster.

I tried to sound like one. "Okay, guys, listen up." I was a little surprised how quickly I got their attention. "Before we chow, let's try on the costumes in case we need to make any last-minute alterations."

Mara opened the cedar closet and handed out the costumes. There was a lot of chatter and laughter. Jon and Brian were scarecrows with straw hats and orange plastic pumpkin heads. Jeff and Alison were skeletons with rubber skull masks that completely covered their heads, and Mara and Spike were witches with pointy black hats and hideous crone masks.

The big noise came when Vandal and I climbed into loose-fitting green jumpsuits with big green papier-mâché masks that fit over our heads like deep-sea divers' helmets. Mara and I had spent days making the hairless green heads with red-rimmed eyes.

Everybody got it right away, but it was Jon, of course, who said it. "Looks just like you."

"The Chemo Kid," said Vandal, his voice muffled. "World's ugliest superhero."

Alison clapped her hands, and Brian and Spike high-fived, but Jeff and Jon looked a little embarrassed. I let it pass. There are some things you just can't explain, like tumor humor. It's a location joke. You have to be there.

While they ate, I went over the plan, following the outline taped to the mirror.

At eight fifteen, Jon and Jeff would leave in the Jag to pick up their dates, Joanie Kim and Laura

Marino, planning to arrive at the school gym by nine.

Mara and I would leave the house at eight forty-five and go directly to the dance, where we would mingle, take off our masks as often as possible, and make sure everyone knew we were there.

At nine forty-five, Vandal, Spike, Brian and Alison would leave the house and head toward the school, aiming to pull the van behind the gym at ten.

We would then change places with them. Laura and Joanie, who were in on some of the plan, would guide them into the dance. Jon, Jeff, Mara and I would drive the van back to the parking lot, take off our costumes and leave in our own cars.

"We'll need about forty-five minutes," I said. "Make yourselves as visible as possible without taking off your masks. Any questions?"

"What if people talk to us?" asked Alison.

"Keep moving, dance as much as possible."

"Problem right there," said Vandal. "I've danced semi-pro. I got trophies I haven't polished yet. Give it away right there."

"No one's ever noticed me on the floor." I liked the cool, unafraid sound of my voice. "Do your best. Let 'em think cancer makes you a better dancer."

"Everybody'll want one," said Brian.

"What if we need to talk to you guys?" asked Spike.

"You'll have the number of the phone in Jon's car.

143

We'll have no way to call you. We thought about walkie-talkies, but we didn't want to take the chance of being overheard."

"When do you come back?" asked Spike.

"We're shooting for eleven, just before people start peeling off. Take turns going out back to look for the van. We'll all meet after midnight at the Athenian Diner in Wallbrook. It's on your maps."

I went through it all one more time, probably more to hear my own voice than anything else. I had Jeff and Jon tell Brian and Alison a little bit about Laura and Joanie and then I reviewed the routes from the house to the school and to the diner in Wallbrook.

"Any questions?"

"What if something goes wrong?" asked Jeff.

"Doc Bini's door is always open," said Spike.

When Jeff looked puzzled, Brian said, "We don't worry about anything except cancer."

"If there aren't any more questions, Jeff and Jon better take off."

"Wait," said Alison. "We should all hold hands and share good thoughts and white light."

I thought at least Spike would have something smart to say, but she put her hands right into the circle, trying to touch as many other hands as possible, just like everyone else.

It felt good.

22

COACH BURG WAS STANDING at the door as Mara and I walked into the gym. "You're not coming in here with that getup," he snarled. "Making fun of a poor sick—"

I lifted off my mask.

"You!" He whipped off his varsity cap and slapped it over his heart. "I always admired your guts, Ted."

We made sure people noticed us. The costumes got a lot of attention. Some of the teachers and chaperones were offended, even after they saw it was me. Cancer makes people uncomfortable. But most of the kids laughed. "Outrageous," they called as we danced past. "Radical."

We danced over to Jon and Jeff and Joanie and Laura. Ace and Scribe seemed nervous.

"Relax, guys, the Pack's on the case."

"They were always flaky," said Jon.

"This is no game," said Jeff.

"Where's Roger and Tank?" I asked.

"Usual place."

Guys were milling around outside the bathroom when we got there. "Better not go—" someone shouted, but I led Jon and Jeff right through the crowd.

Tank and a huddle of football players were up against one white tile wall, passing a bottle and waiting while Roger and the twin goons spread out their drugstore.

"Now I know what *déjà vu* means," I said.

"Would you repeat that?" asked Jeff.

"What are you guys doing in here?" growled Tank. He was dressed up to look like a cross between Miss Piggy and that country-western singer with the pillowy chest. He had a blond wig, and the front of his white gown was stuffed with two footballs. It was cut so low, you could see his hairy chest. Why do the biggest apes always like to dress like women, red lipstick and all? Have to ask Dr. Wallabini some day.

"Clever. Costume." Roger rolled up. He was dressed as a homeless beggar. He even had a dirty paper coffee cup in his hand. "Who are you?"

I pulled off my paper head.

"I don't get it." Tank shrugged and looked around. The other players shrugged.

"Get this." I struggled to keep my voice down to a roar. "You humps are history."

Tank and Roger glanced at each other.

Roger said. "Do you have something. On your mind. Fred?" He nodded at Tank. "Let's take. A meeting."

Tank grabbed one arm, Roger the other. I felt the ice dots form under their fingers. They started steering me toward the stalls.

"Hold it," shouted Jeff. "Fred needs to take his medicine. Right now. There's a nurse outside waiting to give him a shot."

"We'll bring him right back, of course," said Jon.

"Get lost," growled Tank.

"We need to talk. To Fred alone."

"Be careful," said Jeff. "What he's got is very new. Highly contagious. His veins could explode if you squeeze too hard."

"It's nine fifty-six," said Jon, tapping his wristwatch.

Roger and Tank pushed me against the tile of the back wall. I heard the water in the sink fall in small explosions. I saw the bubbles of sweat between the black hairs of Roger's little moustache. Smelled Tank's perfume. Perfume?

"Listen close, Fred," said Roger. "This is. Your last warning. Tank and I. Like the way things are."

"If you don't," said Tank, "you better find yourself another high school."

"And your father," said Roger. "Better find himself. Another town."

"Or maybe your mother," growled Tank, "will have to find herself a new husband and son."

"Now you." My voice boomed off the tiles. "Pay attention to me."

I grabbed Tank first, around his waist, and lifted him over my head.

"Put me down," he screamed.

"You bet." I carried him into one of the stalls and lowered him into the toilet bowl. "Don't you move."

It was great. Tank stood there petrified, his mouth open, afraid to move a muscle. I had an urge to flush, but I controlled it.

Roger hadn't moved—he was frozen with surprise. It was easy to pick him up and carry him into another stall. "My good shoes," he whimpered as I lowered him into the toilet bowl.

I actually considered letting him take them off, that's how much of a wimp I am, but Jon hollered, "Nine fifty-nine," and I dropped him with a plop.

"Don't you even dream about twitching a muscle until I say so," I roared. "I'll be back to check every so often."

The football huddle and the twins parted silently as I led Jon and Jeff out of the bathroom.

"Why couldn't you have done that on the football field?" asked Jeff.

"Saved us a lot of trouble," said Jon.

"Because it wasn't right."

"Right?" asked Jeff.

"Later," I said.

The crowd outside the bathroom stared at us.

"Go on in," I said.

Mara was waiting behind the gym, pacing and checking her watch. "Ten oh one. Where are they?"

"Mutants run on their own time," said Jeff.

"That's no way to talk about them," snapped Mara.

"It's The Game, the stupid game," said Jon.

I heard the van a block away. "Here we go," I said.

Spike braked the van in a storm of gravel. "Almost didn't make it."

"There's a cop back there," said Brian, climbing out, "who thinks Freddy's public enemy number one."

"Sergeant Durie," said Alison. "He's stopping cars. He's looking for you."

"I'm almost impressed," said Vandal.

"Don't get your hopes up," said Spike.

"Tonight," said Vandal, "I may be able to improve his reputation."

"Don't forget," said Mara, "we still have to go to this school."

"After this night," said Spike, twirling her broomstick, "when they think of witch they'll think of you."

"'Witch' is almost the word I'd use for you, Spike," said Alison sweetly.

"Ten four," said Jon.

"Gotta go," I said. "There are two guys standing in toilets. The one dressed like a bimbo is captain of the football team, the bum is the dope dealer."

"Tank and Roger, I know all about them," said Vandal. "Consider their careers down the drain."

"We'd better go," said Jon. "Ten five."

"Showtime," said Brian.

Vandal said, "Make us proud, Chemo Kid."

23

"**H**OW DO YOU FEEL?"

"A little nervous." She checked her watch. "Ten twenty. How do you feel?"

"Icy. Wired. Sharp. You switched toothpaste. Cinnamon."

"It's so amazing."

"It could get annoying though."

"No, I mean us, together, doing this thing. And you. The cold fire." She waited until I pulled the van off the road at the edge of the iron fence and we both took off our costumes before she touched my hand and said, "You're really a hero. We couldn't have done this without you."

"We haven't done it yet."

"We wouldn't have gotten this far. Look, Fred." I heard the click of dryness in her throat. "You don't need to go in with me."

"We already decided."

"If anything happened, I mean, in your condition . . ."

"I've got powers, you know I've . . ." My voice trailed off. I thought of Tank and Roger standing in the toilets. Could it all be part of a plot to make me feel good? Like ten-year diaries and invitations to a dance?

The ice dots and my self-confidence began to melt. All a crazy chemo dream.

"You've got powers, Freddy." She squeezed my hand. "Powers inside you that make you a good person, a good friend, someone who can inspire others to—"

Jeff honked the Jag's horn, twice, the signal. Ten twenty-two. In the rearview mirror, I saw Jeff give us the thumbs-up. Behind him, in the backseat, I could see Jon hunched over the phone and the laptop in the backseat. He was smiling. He'd jacked into the Sinclair net; he'd be able to read out the code on the electronic gate and open it for us when we were ready to go out again.

"Let's go." I jumped out of the car.

I heard the truck's gears shift a block away. We crouched and ran along the fence toward the gate. I smelled chemicals, felt airborne microscopic toxic particles brush my skin. Or thought I did.

Maybe it didn't matter.

"It'll be opening in a second," I said.

"How can you tell?"

"I can hear the hum."

The gate slid open and the truck appeared out of the night, headlights glaring. We ducked until it passed us, then followed it into the yard. The gate slid shut behind us.

We stayed in a shadow while the truck turned and backed into the squat building as the corrugated metal door rolled up with a screechy whine that needled into my brain. It blotted out all thought, but I followed Mara across the yard.

Men came out on the loading platform. We dove under the truck.

We were lying very close to each other. I could feel her breath on my cheek, hear her heartbeat, smell her new perfume, Pine Needles. They were all like little melodies running through the blary brass and the brain-crunching thump, the stink of chemicals, the thud of heavy footsteps, the clank and grind of machinery. The panting of dogs.

I nudged Mara. "We can't go in. They've got dogs."

"Got to get the samples from inside the plant, before they put the masking agents in."

"You go alone."

"I thought you—" She heard them, a low warning growl. The dogs knew we were here. Her eyes widened.

"I'll keep 'em busy."

"No, you'll get—"

I rolled out from under the trucks. My voice boomed, "Hey, doggie, doggie."

There were two of them, long sleek dark shapes in the dim light of the yard. They pawed the earth, barked and strained at their leashes.

A man shouted, "Hit the spots," and the lights mounted on top of the building and on the fence posts flared, blinding me. I could feel their heat, hear their buzz, smell the cooking glass of their bulbs. I concentrated to blot them out and find Mara. Cinnamon and Pine Needles. The rhythm of her heart. Dark hair whipping around the corner of the loading platform.

She was inside.

Okay.

Time for the Chemo Kid—or whatever he is—to go out in a blaze of glory.

I ran into the warmth of the spotlights. It was like running out on a stage. I threw up my arms and turned twice and bowed. Let them think I was crazy.

Wasn't I?

An electronic bullhorn thundered, "YOU ARE ON PRIVATE PROPERTY."

I began to run. Not toward anything, not away from anything, just to run, to move, to feel the breeze whipping against my face, to feel the power pump up through my legs and into my body.

"STOP WHERE YOU ARE!"

I'd never felt so strong, so fast, so filled with energy.

"THIS IS YOUR LAST WARNING. WE WILL RELEASE THE GUARD DOGS."

I roared, "CATCH ME IF YOU CAN."

A baseball cap, TOP GUN, appeared under the lights, followed by half a dozen caps, crunching footsteps all around, the light, quick patter of the dogs.

The Chemo Kid runs, jumps, dances in the blazing light. Two dark forms streak at his chest, he ducks beneath them, they collide in midair and collapse in a heap, whimpering. Men surround him, grab at his arms. He twists out of their grasp, spins away from their hands. One grabs him from behind. He throws him over his shoulder.

Sirens in the distance.

I don't know how long it lasted—a minute? an hour?—but I felt as though I could go on forever, no one could stop me, no one could bring me down. The dogs slunk away, the men backed off, I was alone again, spinning and jumping in my insane dance.

The Chemo Kid never quits.

The Chemo Kid never dies.

Cinnamon and Pine Needles. She was out of the building, running toward the gate. Two honks of the Jag's horn. They've cracked the code, the gate was opening. Just another few seconds.

Police cars pulled up, blocking the open gate. She would never get out now.

I sprinted across the yard, my feet barely touching the ground. I caught up with her in a long shadow near the fence.

"I've got it," she said, waving the vials. "How do we get out?"

"Climb on my back," I said.

"What?"

"Just do it," I roared.

She wrapped her arms around my chest and her legs around my waist and pressed her face against my back. She didn't feel any heavier than a backpack.

"Hang on."

The Chemo Kid moves like a Hovercraft, never quite touching the ground, but never quite flying until he reaches the fence. Does he leap in a single bound, does he fly over it, does he walk up one side of the fence and down the other? Even those who have seen it with their own eyes will argue among themselves forever. And the Kid isn't talking. Maybe he doesn't know for sure either.

"Freddy, look out, the reservoir."

Does he swim the silvery waters, does he knife

across like a ghostly canoe, a dolphin, a submarine?
Who knows? The Chemo Kid knows only that he is
on the other side, and both he and Scattergood are
very wet. He feels her slide off with relief. He is sud-
denly very tired.

"Freddy, how did you do it?"

"I don't know." I really didn't.

"It's so hard to believe. Do you realize what this
means?"

"An end to pollution in Nearmont?" I sat down in
the soft grass.

"That's just for starters. Freddy, you've got super
powers." The barolium filled her eye sockets, the
hollows in her cheeks, the ebony of her hair. I
wished I had the energy to kiss her. "You'll be able
to shut down polluters all over the country, the
world. You'll be able to help people in so many
ways. You'll be able to—"

"I'm really whipped." I hated the whine in my
voice.

"Just one more fence."

No way. The energy had oozed out through my
toes and the ice dots were melted. The last fence.
On the other side was the reservoir parking lot. A
short walk to the van. Freedom.

A car pulled into the parking lot and nailed us
with its lights. I tried to think. To focus. But I'd
lost it. So close.

A rope ladder came over the fence and slapped

on our side. Mara pushed me ahead of her. Step by slow and painful step. At the top, I almost slipped but I managed to get down.

Sergeant Durie was waiting for us on the other side. "I know what you kids did."

I put out my wrists. "She didn't have anything to do with this. Just take me. I won't break your cuffs."

"This is no movie," growled Sergeant Durie. "You're a real hero, kid. We're gonna get them."

"Get them?" asked Mara.

"The Mayor, the Sinclair Ecosystems guys. They were running an illegal toxic waste disposal plant. I couldn't get my chief to make the case. But I figured you kids would break in and we could follow and collect our own evidence." He patted our backs. "Never could have done it without you kids. But you broke the law."

"Sometimes you've got to break something," I said.

"Still a wise guy." Sergeant Durie chuckled. "Need a lift?"

I spotted the Jag cruising along the county road. "We're covered."

"Okay now, beat it before the chief sees you. Any problems, just call me."

He got in his police car and drove away.

"I thought he was going to take us in," said Mara.

"You can never tell about Bang," I said. "He's almost as unpredictable as the Pack."

158

24

JOANIE AND LAURA were pacing nervously behind the gym. They ran back inside when we pulled up in the van. The Jag was right behind us. The Pack poured out a moment later, chattering and laughing. We made the switch fast, no time for press conferences, but Brian threw me a thumbs-up and I got a glimpse of Vandal with his mask off. He looked very pleased with himself.

Tank and Roger were still standing in the toilets. It looked as though they hadn't twitched a muscle since I left.

They were like exhibits in some weird zoo. Guys walked in and out of the bathroom, laughing at them, making remarks, throwing wads of wet towel at them.

No one was afraid of them anymore.

"Fred. Please," said Roger. "Enough is. Enough."

"Gimme a break," whined Tank.

"We'll do everything. You said."

"Promise," whined Tank.

What did I say? What did Vandal say for me? I stood there, wiped out, trying to think.

Jon thought for me. "Repeat what Fred told you."

"No more. Selling drugs. Community service. Go around to the schools. Tell them what's bad. About dope. How I made money. Off them."

Jon nodded. "And what did Fred say would happen if you didn't?"

"He'd get me."

"How?"

"Snap my legs. Like a rusty tailpipe."

That sounded like Vandal.

Jon looked at Tank. "What did he tell you?"

"No more booze or steroids. Play clean," said Tank.

"What else?" asked Jon.

"That's it," said Tank.

"What about the school paper?" said Jeff.

"He didn't say anything about that."

"He certainly did," said Jeff. Jon and I looked at each other. "He told you to make sure that the school paper gets its funding. Fred wants the next issue in a week."

160

"How can I do that?"

"Easy," said Jeff. "Tell Coach Burg if there's no school paper, there's no football team. They'll find the money. You got that?"

"Anything," said Tank.

"And while you're at it," said Jon, "don't forget the Computer Team."

"Or the Ecology Club," I said.

Coach Burg was waiting for us outside the bathroom. "You must be tired," he said to me. "After what you did tonight."

A flutter of fear. "How did you know?"

"Saw it with my own eyes. You deserved first prize." He touched the peak of his varsity cap. "Especially for those Latin dances. And that witch of yours—"

"Tank wants to talk to you," said Jeff.

"Where is he?"

"On the toilet," said Jon.

"Actually," said Jeff, "he is in the toilet."

"Write that down," said Jon.

Mara and I took one last turn around the dance floor with our masks off to make sure everyone saw us before we slipped out and drove to the diner. The Pack had a big back table loaded with pizza.

I don't remember too much of what went on, except it lasted a long time and there was a lot of laughing and hugging. Jon and Alison disappeared into a corner for a while. Sometime before Mara drove me home at dawn, Vandal put his arm around me and pulled my head right up against his earring. "Any time, Chemo Kid, any place, for any reason, you need me, just call."

"You're the leader of the Pack," I said.

"And the Pack will be back."

Mara had to help me out of the car and into my house. She looked into my eyes and put her hands on my neck and leaned forward to kiss me.

Just before our lips met, she said, "Your neck, Freddy. The lump's gone."

25

DR. WALLABINI JUMPED UP when I walked into his office. I hadn't seen him in two months, since he'd stopped the chemo. "I have such good news." I thought he was going to hug me. "NED."

"My name's Fred."

"I know that, Frad. NED means No Evidence of Disease."

"I'm cured?"

He knocked on his wooden desk. "I never use that word. You are clean. You are clear. Very encouraging." He stepped back and looked me over. "But you haven't changed one bit."

"I'm the same guy I always was."

"After two months you should be looking more like your old self. Your hair should be growing in. Not so puffy, so green." He sat down in his big chair. "Unless . . ."

"Is something wrong?"

"It really worked." He began to grin. "The experimental hormone really worked. It persuaded your natural defenses to exert superhuman effort."

"Its what I've been trying to tell you. I have superhuman powers."

"Of course. Your powers will be yours forever, Frad. You will always be a superhero."

"You're sure?"

"Of course. Gold and silver may be stolen, but never inner strength."

I could tell he wasn't getting it. "I mean, for real."

"Real is here." He tapped his head. "You are going to be a chapter in my book, Frad. Never have I had a patient who did such a good job of reinventing, of taking control of his destiny."

"Could we please close the door." The galaxy of ice dots appeared. "Just this once?"

"My door is always open, Frad. That was part of your getting well." He looked so proud of himself. "When my research is published, there will be shrink-raps in every cancer center in America. The link between the mind and the body will be established beyond—"

"It wasn't all in my head, Dr. Wallabini."

"What's the matter with your voice?"

164

"It's part of what I've been trying to tell you."

"What are you doing?" His voice was rising.

The power surged into my arms and turned my hands into steel clamps. I lifted the huge wooden desk.

"Frad?" It was a squeak.

I lifted the desk over my head. "Could you listen to me, please?"

"Wait," he said, "until I close my door."

We talked for a long time. People pounded on the door, the phone rang, messages blinked through his computer, but Dr. Wallabini never took his eyes off me, except to make sure his tape recorder was running, or to make a note.

He asked a lot of questions. He wanted to know exactly when I first noticed the powers, what events or emotions triggered the ice dots, was I stronger right after a treatment, were my powers increasing, how long did they last each time. I couldn't answer most of the questions as precisely as he wanted.

"I wish you had taken notes."

"I would've if you'd believed me in the first place."

He sighed. "What a loss to science."

"Unless I started keeping notes now."

"Too late. I will immediately begin a new course of drugs for you that will purge your system of the hormone's effect. Your natural defenses will return to normal, and you will look like your old self."

165

"And my powers?"

"You don't need them."

"How about for what you might learn? For your research, your book?"

"I can't leave you like this, Frad."

"What about other kids with cancer? Look, Dr. Wallabini, we know that humans operate at only a fraction of their physical and mental capacities—"

"How do we know that?"

I didn't want to say we know because Jon Park says so. "—and if you could raise that fraction you'd be in Nobel Prize territory, not to mention patents worth billions."

He took a deep breath. "I am not a business-man, Frad, I am a scientist. Like the hero of *The Incredible Hulk*."

"What if I refuse to take any more drugs? What if I just say no?"

"Don't you want to be normal?"

"What's normal? Being invisible? Being here, we think?"

"Pardon me?"

"You'd have to have been there, Doc Bini."

I opened the door. The hall was filled with nurses and patients who had never seen the door closed before. I pushed through the crowd and walked out onto the terrace. I think he tried to follow me, but the crowd swallowed him.

Be normal. Fred Bauer again. That wasn't so bad. I'd made good friends, I'd had adventures, I'd discovered things inside myself I didn't know were there. I'd been a leader. I had a girlfriend.

Just say no, and be swollen and hairless and green.

And be a superhero. We think.

I leaned over the terrace wall and looked through the iron fence at the ships in the harbor. Beyond them, the ocean met the sky. It's a big world; there's lots to do. And I don't even know yet what the Chemo Kid could become capable of doing.

Just how super could my powers get? Could I leap over a building, knock down a building, see through a building?

I bounced on the balls of my feet, rose ten feet in a single bound to the top of the iron fence. I hung from the bar one-handed and closed my eyes against the cool breeze off the ocean.

Could the Chemo Kid learn to fly?

Be great.